Songs on the Water

stories by

Jackson Culpepper

WAYFARER BOOKS

BERKSHIRE MOUNTAINS, MASSACHUSETTS

WAYFARER BOOKS
WWW.WAYFARERBOOKS.ORG

All Rights Reserved
Published in 2023 by Wayfarer Books
Cover Design and Interior Design by Les Browning
Cover Image © Lane Gore
TRADE PAPERBACK 978-1-956368-64-2

10 9 8 7 6 5 4 3 2 1

Look for our titles in paperback, ebook,
and audiobook wherever books are sold.
Wholesale offerings for retailers available through Ingram.

PO Box 1601, Northampton, MA 01060

860.574.5847 | info@homeboundpublications.com

HOMEBOUNDPUBLICATIONS.COM & WAYFARERBOOKS.ORG

contents

The Birth and Immolation of a Southern God at the Hands of All

It is said that we become the monsters we fight; then what great beast did General Sherman see that so transmogrified him?

–ANONYMOUS HISTORIAN, DRUNK

Our Boy, halfway through another day full of nothing, took another drink, swore, and lit a bottle rocket from where he sat, watching it arc over the yard and land sputtering in the lake. He did this because he was still a boy and should have been a young man by now, but instead still had those two words of boyhood in his mind and in his blood: *fuck it.* This product of his environment cranked his father's white golf cart, taking the rockets and the beer, loading everything into the wire caddy and took to the road—Our Boy was angry because anger was under everything around him: anger in the steel of the railroad tracks that divided the town, anger in the eyes of the stone Confederate of the square who opposed the ongoing war from the north, anger in the bones of the buried malcontented dead and of the slaves below them and of the Muskogee down below everybody and if there was a devil below them, he didn't have to do much.

But it's beer and fireworks! OB and his folks lived in one of the newer houses in the Valhalla subdivision, where everyone pronounced the name with the first two A's drawled out to all hell. Some of the houses were huge bungalows while others were brick, just like the rich ones in town; the owners hadn't made the creative jump to lake-rich, they just saw the first thing they came to and called it "rich" and stuck with that. OB hates them, but for a good reason: he's never felt at home there.

He crossed the empty highway to one of the dirt roads lined with viney heaviness. OB reached back and lit bottle rockets, first in the wire basket which sent them off like chaff from a fighter jet and then, one foot on the wheel, OB aimed with one hand and lit with the other and found out he was pretty good at that missilery (perhaps because his people were good, and knew it, at all missilery.) Few more yards and he let a cow have it broadsides, boom! Pop! against its steak parts and it ran crooning, like a dumb crying kid. OB aimed and shot, aimed and shot—one rocket hit a mule, but the damn stupid thing didn't move, didn't make a sound. OB took this as an accusation of impotence.

(Of the words above this is the most important: *Our,* capitalized. Because all is one, maybe, or because ole Faulkner said the past isn't even gone and plenty of bullets have proved him right, and ole Heschel said some are guilty but all are responsible. And is an Our Boy made of words any different, in our hearts, from one of flesh?)

OB pulled into his friend Wade's drive and shot a bottle rocket at his front door. *Boom! Pop!*

"The fuck," Wade said. He came out in cut-off khakis (same as OB) and a striped shirt washed too many times (OB left shirtless). It goes without saying they're both wearing destroyed ball caps, Wade's for the Braves and OB's for the Dawgs, *sic 'em, roo roo roo roo.* "You knocked a divot in the door, you asshole."

"You can't tell from the street."

"Like hell you can't. You got beer?"

"Get in, we got to find Joe."

"He's at baseball camp."

"How about Josh?"

"Probably home. Hey, give me one of those beers."

OB lit a rocket at him and Wade hit the floor and it buzzed off and smacked into one of the neighbor's palmettos where it popped, blowing dried leaves through the air and the stick part stuck, hanging out of the bush like a tiny erection. The visual was lost, for once, on the boys.

Wade got in and drank, OB pulled out of the drive and drank, and they cruised the Scenic Route (actual name of the road) and drank.

While the big green self-consciousness monster (it looks like a Muppet with double-sided razor blades for its teeth) chewed on OB's legs, Wade developed a conversation about the video games he rented from the store in town, like he always did (that is, the kid always rented video games in town. He's played all sixty-three titles they have for the PlayStation, from the good sneaking, fighting and role-playing ones down to the shitfests: the generic tankers and ones where you run hacking through levels that each look exactly the same. In fact, he's the reason you can never check out the good games, because odds are Wade Taylor got there before you and he's in with the dudes that work there and gets those suckers before they even get reshelved.

He's going to wind up rich enough to live in the part of Albany, Georgia where you enjoy living in Albany, Georgia. And since Wade plays a ton of these games, and since they're about the most interesting things that happen to Wade during the summer, it's all he talks about.) Too bad for OB, he realized back at *Mortal Kombat* on Sega that he failed at all such things and gave up.

So the two protagonists (heroes) roll down the back roads, those mythical, beautiful, ageless back roads that country singers turn into something beautiful but these kids—nah, just look at it: there's a once-white golf cart careening like a space shuttle launch in its own dust and from this golf cart come booze belches, spare cans, a steady lecture on the boss fight with Psycho Mantis and how it frustrated the hell out of everybody who played it, except for OB, who as he knows is ≤ (everybody -1). If you're literal here, also imagine a big green Muppet being dragged along, dust collecting in its felt, as it gnaws OB's leg. And, never far from the story, the *boom! Pop!* of stray rockets that OB's lighting up like a three-pack-a-day man lights up cigarettes—which is, not even meaning to. Fences and farms swirl by on either side, not that Wade and OB pay any attention whatsoever.

Josh's house, framed by tall pines, recalls the White House if all you think about is columns and big. Three stories of open front, Scarlet-waiting-for-Rhett columned porchery, a balcony on each of the upper levels. Two young magnolias flank the alabaster driveway, which weaves its pleasing parabola around a pine straw mound of ferns, bougainvillea, and carefully pruned crepe myrtles. The rest of the arc is immaculate lawn—the lines across it in perfect parallel symmetry. So OB doughnuts the dusty bandwagon right onto the grass.

"Jesus man, first my door then–"

Blasts from the horn, *weemp weemp* and one *boom! Pop*! that whistles into the balcony like it's thinking of buying the place before exploding into the seat of a painted UGA rocker. Josh comes out wearing a goddamn cowboy hat. Not a Stetson but one of those crushed straw gas-station things and it's all you can do not to picture a rebel flag somewhere close by. Of course, Wade and OB instantly made fun of him.

"Tex, the fuck?"

"It's cool man, I wore it to the party last night and Katie danced with me." (Thus: Josh= teenage boy + money + jackass cowboy hat. Further, Josh + Katie = success. Therefore, teenage boy + money + jackass cowboy hat + Katie = success. OB is trying to figure this stuff out.)

"Get in."

"Where are we going?" John Wayne asked.

OB, finding no reasonable response, knocked a rocket over Josh's head close enough to singe the loose straw bits sticking off the top. Josh climbed in.

(THE PAST: The first known Georgia hillbilly party to occur, at least with European men most of them from English penal colonies, happened some time in the Jacksonian era and, though a fledgling effort, had enough rum and homebrew floating around that the boys figured out, sure enough, that it was funny to load powder and wadding and shoot your ramrod out of your rifle. On about the third occasion of this, just as Jeroboam Lincoln (he changed his name in '65) was figuring out how to then make the ramrod explode once it was out, a tribe of justifiably pissed-off Muskogee (You would be pissed too. Imagine having these guys for neighbors who were jack-asses to begin with, plus their daddies kicked your daddies off land you'd lived on since Buzzard raised the mountains, and the jackassery hadn't let up since. The tribe was patient for a long time but in the end they faced the damned-if-you-do choice: get pushed by the interlopers to the ends of the earth, or get up and kill the bastards.) came across the river quietly enough to sneak past the guards better than Solid Snake could've, and started sniping arrows into some motherfuckers. The Georgia boys, they grabbed up their rifles but the things were only loaded with ramrods, plus Riley's who thought it would be funny to load his wife's nicest pair of drawers into it and see if they took shape when they came out. So boom boom boom, and three-foot ramrods flew past the Muskogee, who as a body turned toward the missiles as they wobbled by, and in one voice, in Muskogee, said,

"The fuck?"

This gave Riley enough time to save the day by launching Mrs. Riley's drawers. They inflated and floated like the ghost of his wife's ass. Besides making the Muskogee think this was some serious Crow medicine, they couldn't see, so large was the garment, and that gave the Georgia boys time to grab up pistols where they had them stashed and, as we know from brutal history, *touchdown, sic 'em, roo roo roo roo.*

The tradition, thus established, slugged its drunken way through teary renditions of "Lorena," didn't work so well against Sherman. They lost. Who knows the full sum of what they lost, or its quality? It's not a question for pity but for reckoning. And anyway here's the thing: the Georgia boys, they're sore losers. Like a dog that, once kicked, snarls on all. Like screaming Watson in front of the capitol.

Five generations later, Our Boys of the same stock forge ahead.)

Josh climbed onto the back of the golf cart, which was a bad decision since if the driving didn't kill him the rockets might. He held on with one hand on the back bumper and the other on his hat (very important because hat = girls). OB, for his part, was trying desperately to knock that stupid hat away without appearing to. He swerved, throttled, braked, but each time he looked back there it was, spray-painted straw, brand new and beat up as hell. So he veered down an embankment.

The tires of the golf cart left the earth and hung in zero-gravity for 2.67 seconds. During this time, Josh floated up off the back bumper, his hat floated off his head, Wade gripped the roof for dear life, and OB cracked his next beer and shot three of his biggest rockets to clear the path. Shuffle and re-shuffle, they landed with one kid across the neck rest, another half out the windshield (or where it would be) and OB holding on like a sailor to the mizzenmast.

Skidding to a halt, they groaned, moved, checked if this was heaven or hell, and the smoke cleared. Before them was a wide yard, bungalow (the actual, small kind,) and an enclosed dock. They ran.

"First one gets it," called Wade.

"Wait up," said Josh, just before OB kicked his leg out from under him (sporting or mean? They went running to the dock, flung open the door and there, shining, beautiful, three Yamaha waverunners rested in canvas moorings, two doubles and a four-man hoss. The boys, under OB's eye, transferred the beer, rockets, hat. Most of the booty they loaded onto the big boy, that aquatic Percheron, plus just enough on the little ones to get by.

So they saddled up, manned the winches, lowered into the arena and coughed the beasts to life. Blue gas fumes barked out of the nostrils, the water churned as they leaped to a lope out of the slough and into the Lake proper.

What freedom! Cause even falling off the damned things you couldn't get hurt, it was only *ker-splash* and swim back to it (they can swim, right?) So first thing, Josh and Wade started jousting on them, flying at sixty over the smoothest water they could find, rocket-lances skidding up the fiberglass snouts and exploding, *boom! Pop!*, behind them. OB ordered a raid. In close formation, under the old Georgia flag (the old one still with the stars and bars), they approached one:

Pontoon boat, containing: Mom, Pop, Sister age 16, her boyfriend Andy on the cell phone screaming to be heard on the water, little Billy and Bobby tubing on a red-white-and-blue wedge-shaped thing behind. Their speed: 15 mph. Their cargo: Coca-Cola, Zero bars, the .38 Pop kept under the seat.

Flight of the Valkyries. OB, point, fired the first volley overheard. Wade and Josh flanked opposite. Circling like Mongols outside the range of Pop's .38 (now out and firing, with his curses, and his wife pulling in Billy and Bobby as from a burning house) the boys rode in one at a time, high speed, launching all the rockets they could in a number of seconds, then back out of range, and the next boy went, and so forth. Of course OB was the best at this. His runs launched a dozen or more decent rockets at the family boat, denting the hull. Josh could only manage two or three, his hat flapping on its chin-strap. Wade, not to be outdone, figured a way to launch a whole pack of the tiny 24/$1 ones like hornets, bedeviling Pop's careful aim with his last two bullets and poor Sis couldn't hear Andy at all.

Pop called by way of failing authority, "Is there no respect left?"

OB and Co. answered truthfully, "No sir."

"Then answer, at least, why this violence and rage?"

"Because why not, sir?"

"That is insufficient."

OB rode close, trimming the bow high, his pale body taut and the confidence of mad youth flashing in his eyes. "Perhaps, sir, because each generation must destroy the last," OB said. "Perhaps because your generation surrendered to that marching army of boxes now lining the highway which strangled to death our lovely brick downtown, which may actually have been real. Surrendered all that which was real for comfort and large televisions and those damned big houses. Surrendered rebellion itself because instead of the sword and gun, you chose the assassin's knife of decency." OB said, "Because, sir, this land burns."

Josh and Wade laughed with barbarian glee at the cratered, burning, listing craft. Pop its lone, blackened defender. The boys war-whooped as the wreck bubbled into the water, Pop saluting to Taps.

They sped across the lake, OB in lead with the other two cutting his wake. Other jetski's came along and left with missiles hurling through their rooster tails or our heroes gave chase, threatening to ride them down; old men in fishing boats received the empties from the C.S.S. OB; all the skiers, kneeboarders, wakeboarders, slollumers, and tubers got their ski ropes cut; until—until . . .

(NOW: We will peer into OB's brain, which, lacking a fully developed frontal lobe due to his age, claws at itself to make some sense of what he's doing. He knows it's in some way for a capitol-S South, but also for Georgia, and for this land he knows and, if he'll admit it, loves, and for his friends but in large part for himself. For his anger, perhaps, out of some irrational vengeance—but there needs to be more to it, he thinks, and runs raw the gears of his mind making himself signify something.

What is left of the South for OB to raise again? We won't delude ourselves that white supremacy, while not articulated, doesn't hang like a fascist banner at the back of his thoughts—and yet the song in his head has been Pastor Troy's very own "Ain't No Mo Play in GA," not to mention those thoughts expressed in "O Father" which OB has spent whole evenings contemplating over cigarettes pilfered from his father. OB copied in his notebook for further consideration these lines—

No way to win cause we are in for the ride of our lives

I was writing this shit I had to wipe my eyes

Cause this is chaos they after us we'll never succeed

—because somehow in the contemplation of it this white kid in a three-thousand square foot house felt the *same way*. OB understood it to be true for himself on a level he couldn't yet comprehend. *But also* he felt the first stirrings of compassion for someone else's suffering he'd ever felt in his life. Every gun-blast of the Pastor's ethos built to this in OB's mind: weeping, desperation, loss of hope. Here lay the beating beaten heart of all the rage and bravado. And that defeat or its admission made OB yet more angry: angry about everything he understood Pastor Troy to be angry about. Angry too, on a deeper level, about his own complicity in that oppression. Angry at his helplessness, angry at his shame, and ashamed.

And so OB has carried in his heart that growing star of his shame. We could say it, that he's a sore loser. The ancient wisdom says *Never give a sword to a man who can't dance*; OB fundamentally cannot dance. Yet he lives in a country bristling with swords.)

The Independence Day barge was a moss-covered hunk of steel, lashed with cables to old hollow barrels, styrofoam leaking in spores from underneath. Each year it tolled the bells of fire and ooh and aah to remind our nation that it was born shooting at people and survived the same way. Each year a dozen of the oldest game wardens towed it out. The pontoon always came to its spot and never needed an anchor, it was so conditioned. Then professional ooh-and-aah artists from Atlanta or Macon loaded it with cordite magnificence, ferrying more and more on until its flat deck floated only inches above the water. It was to this discovery, loaded and ready, that Our Boys (why not go ahead and make them family?) came.

OB hauled alongside and hopped from his mount to the deck. None of the fireworks looked like those he was used to: no bright colors, no pictures, just blackened tubes and wires. The only difference between any of them was their bore sizes. They were bolted to long sheets of plywood, one along each of the square pontoon's sides and OB looked around him, judging range and yes—there, within the arc, were the new condo's, the whitewashed neighborhood with its own logo, and the boat club where no few American flags flew and pistol shots filled the air. If the condo's weren't enough, new houseboats, some downright yachts, were moored along a steel pier outside a marina serving frozen drinks. There was endless loud Jimmy Buffet. The panoply was easily enough the symbol if not the substance of all OB believed he hated. For those less tangible objects of his rage, he decided, these would do as well.

While the other boys circled the platform keeping the wardens disturbed, OB lifted the eastern plywood battery. It was very heavy. With a heave he turned all those organ pipes to face exactly where he wanted them, aiming directly at the new neighborhood of condo's. He lifted and turned the other panels toward houseboats, toward the manicured lawn of the park, toward the gathering horde of speedboats bearing fat men and wrinkled women, all the radios playing the same goddamned Jimmy Buffet. He turned each battery out, OB, and made each barrel a ray of his rage. In the setting sun of the birthday of the nation that birthed him, OB lit a last rocket, his biggest one, and cast it down like a thunderbolt.

With brilliant noise and light, pine siding was splintered; corrugated steel was bent and blackened; pleasure boats sank. Flames rose at every turn and crackled against the screams. OB was quite immolated. Josh's hat floated on one of the waves that wasn't burning. You are imagining this, but not enough: everything burned.

OB thus became the weakest god of them all in fiery ranting, pitiful to the last—but it did make a pretty bonfire on the waves: one hell of a party.

Will You Shout
and Will You Cry

The Hateful Shadow passed six days ago. Two days after that another fighterplane crashed into the sand half a mile south of the Rusted Fountain. This one didn't burn.

Only the old men remember the Lake and they have forgotten its name. All they do is forget. We only know the river, what they call the Channel. Up on high ground are the trees: cypress, pine, and hickory, and others we sometimes remember the names of. Then there are those going down to the Lake-bed, mostly fallen and all of them gray as the sky. At night they creak like wounded men and fall. They lean down broken to the bank.

Past the trees are mud flats, littered with the shells of things we once could eat. There are springs of water-soaked brown by Lake poison, bones, sharp flint pieces, and metal cans. Further down the bank is the river. It crawls like Bog did when he desperately drank some of its water—bit by bit, hardly moving. The river is brown with shining trails on top. Long ago we stopped trying to fish it. When the boy Coors ate the slimy fish he died, so we stopped fishing.

We do not go much to the river. For one reason, we cannot drink it. Another reason, the Handbiters live on the other side and come down screaming with their knives. We fought them before and won, but not the second time. No one wants to fight again, after seeing what the Handbiter people do to the wounded. Those dead men's heads watch us from the other bank.

Lincoln has a great pile of arrowheads and he tried to make a club with his biggest and sharpest one at the end. He hit a tree with it and the arrowhead stuck. His hands bled when he tried to pull it out. Months later, when he saw that the tree was keeping it, he took an ax and chopped the tree down.

Sometimes Howlers come from the woods. We can see Longnecks' eyes shining from our campfires.

There are still good plants to eat around the camp. Outboard and his men go east to the town and bring back food, tools, and water. We used to hunt, but there is less and less game. We tried eating alligator meat, but it made the ones that ate it go into a fury like the alligators. We couldn't stop them, and watched as they went out and fought the Handbiters. They fought well until they died from the knives.

Anita figured out how to clean our water. As the springs failed us, she asked for papers and books when Outboard and his foragers went to town. The old men read them to her and taught her to read them and she began cooking the water and letting it drip from a pipe. When she was finished, the water was clear and good. We built her a machine to make more, and dug a pit around it and filled the pit with spikes to keep out our enemies. Sure enough, we found a Howler stuck on one the next day, and let Anita's son kill it with a club. We cooked it and shared it.

The first stories Outboard told us about the town were funny: people running around in bright costumes, dancing when the foragers came in, trying to trade. As time went on, Outboard saw the merchants nailed to billboards. He saw things crawl from under dead cars. He saw flying things. After a while he stopped telling stories about the town.

The foragers come back with less food and water each time. I worried, with the others, what we would do when they came back with nothing. We would have to move and fight the Handbiters and find a new place. Anita would have to abandon her machine. We would be able to look up and see the Things that Fall from the Sky and Kill.

I remember, long ago, that it was a different sky.

When we did finally move, we took down the huts and loaded everything into the back of the truck. Anita burned her machine and was silent. One of the old men worked the levers in the truck while we pulled it along with ropes. Outboard went ahead with his foragers, and by the time we caught up they were fighting the Handbiters. I was selfish and wanted to fight, but I stayed back with the others and shot arrows at the enemy. We killed three or four and they ran. We wanted to scalp them but Outboard turned south and kept going.

We marveled at the Lakebed. People picked up bits of glass and flint, pottery shards. We found the fighterplane. The old men muttered bad luck but we ignored them and dragged out the pilot and took his belongings. Everything is bad luck to the old men.

Things moved in the woods. We looked and saw useless limbs flopping. Then we went back to the truck.

In patches of deep mud, all of us had to pull and push on the truck to get it to move. We wanted to stop but when we looked back and saw Outboard and his men in a lone line behind us, their hands on their guns, we kept moving.

On the third day we came to a dark tower above a wide, deep part of the river. Water flowed underneath the tower. Outboard called us to it, and I was one of the ones who went inside.

There were two large rooms. The machines in them roared and clanked like nothing we had ever heard and it smelled like burning metal. The place was full of bones. The emblem of the Howlers, a wide grimacing face named Exxon, was painted on the wall. Two corpses, well rotten, were chained to the wall. "They starved here," Outboard said, "after the others left." Lincoln kept looking at one of the corpses, which had been a young boy. We broke the lock on a box and found a shotgun and shells, some tools.

"We go east," Outboard said, "to the ocean." And we followed.

I heard Lincoln talk to the old men about what we saw in the tower. He talked like he always does, leaning forward, his body pleading to be understood. Like his words weren't enough. Then I heard one of the old men say, "I will teach you an old thing, a prayer."

The Poet

He was the poet, the one who saw and heard. As far as he knew, the only poet around the lake. He lived in a park bungalow that no ranger seemed to remember, the walls lined with words and words and words, one whole wall of *terza rima* and another of pastorals. So he could feel like he was breathing it.

He had a canoe with two paddles and a dog he never named. Happy lab. This poet woke without a clock, drank weak coffee sometimes from the visitor's center or he'd go to the church by Smoak Bridge and drink church coffee with the pastor there. They got along well, the pastor being a fiction man. He got a kick out of leaving Bukowski next to the prayer books on his shelves and seeing who noticed.

After coffee, the poet went on walks, or scribbled in discarded school notebooks: ideas, lines disconnected from anything sensible, scansion for the calls of water birds and yes, he wrote poems.

They were about the people of the lake—but we can't start there. We must back up and begin at the start if we are to give him justice.

In the beginning, was the Word. The Word stretched twenty miles long by three wide, and was ringed by first-growth pines dropping needles like flurries; live oaks waving Spanish moss like gray shawls; a hundred varieties of thorn bush. Bass and cat and brim and alligators and snakes and monstrous snapping turtles swam in the Word. That was the third day: Word, water; trees; animals (some monsters); and the Georgia sun, a billion-billion watts burning daily in perpetual summer. Each morning so hot you're swimming at eight. The nights were sultry. Midday is hotter than the Hebrews were in Egypt, halfway through building the pyramid. But those sunsets—every night there's a half hour of seraphim singing through the sky. When it rains, the clouds form like beasts plodding through the sky on gray-blue legs of shower. The folks must like it that way.

Then there were churches, clapboard formed from primordial something-or-other, and then the bars, and then people. Just all-a-sudden men in jeans and workboots or shorts and sunglasses or church suits and women in bright swimsuits or gingham sundresses. Together they looked around, dabbed sweat from their brows. They began talking, singing, making love, drinking, and slipping into the water, the Word. Some felt it more than others, but all of them knew it and knowing it, worshiped it, even if it was only on the level of worship approximate to knowing you need to shit, so you shit. They know they need the Word, so they are in the Word. And the Word is with the poet. On his good days, the Word is the poet.

But even a good writer can't do it all day. He sets down the notepad or receipt or whatever he's been composing on and goes about the day. From his shack it takes and hour and a half to paddle to Big John's, three to the dam, and two to the sandbar where everybody stands in the water and drinks their beer. He has many choices.

Wherever he goes, he watches the people—really watches. The poet has the gift of occasional deafness when he can hear English as though it's an unknown language. A fun game, to hear drawling babble between a salty old fella at the bar and a tanned-beyond-the-zero woman, to see them them touching in all the obvious ways. Or to watch two close male friends and see how that intimacy worked when no one would admit that it was intimacy.

And everything in a whole landscape of tip-toeing herons, bass jumping, lathe-turned cypress knees jutting as though from another world. That brown water was the foundation of it all—not sentient but silently omniscient, omnipresent, omnisignificant. Everything comes from that water and will return to it. When all is closed, put away, and forgotten and the grand lake is remade into a spine of river it will still flow alive, long after the poet's dead, if he ever will be.

So he observes, files it away not taxonomized but piled in the junk drawer of his head. With those you know where things are when you need them. Sometimes things show up you'd forgotten about.

The poet knows everyone around the lake. This isn't an exaggeration. He's been (always invited) into every single house, from the poorest trailer to the four-story colonnaced mansion. He's had dinner and supper and tea and been over for beer and you get to know people quick that way. His type especially: he can pick up all the little tics of everybody.

He knows Mac used to play fiddle, and Dale can flatfoot. He knows Marlow never really killed anybody and Henry's still 19 deep down. Are these secrets? No, they are water. One more rush of it in the wake of a boat.

The poet knows things that won't show up in the stories. Behind the fog, outside the sunshine, are desperate places. But isn't there enough else here to keep your attention without the most awful details? Isn't the redemption song good enough music to dance to?

The poet writes so.

He goes by to see Tabitha Guthrie, half for the cooking and half because she's the only one who's read more widely than he. From his shack it's an hour's walk, but she has chamomile tea brewing and yeast rolls baking before he gets there. They begin:

"Did Sutpen represent capitalism or manifest destiny? Or just plain despotism?"

"Did O'Connor really love any of those characters?"

And so forth. Sometimes Tabitha's niece Mabby, brilliant in her own way, joins in, but never as enthusiastically.

On the way back, the poet staggers through the pines where they sway in the torrent wind as it tears from the outer edge of everything he knows and that dirt road—that road long as hell, which terminates in deliverance and all its length is life—burns with more than just the sun, quakes like it might shudder off its grains, mote by mote, until nothing but plain pale white lay bared, bones of this world. He reaches the bungalow, its own walls racked, poems and stories flapping against the boards. He composes, pouring out everything, the tea and crumbs, the needles and dust, his own flesh into a student's discarded notebook with half the pages gone and then—only then—the world happens again.

In the dawning of the first sun-word, there is a beginning.

And in the beginning is the Word.

Like a Burst of Fire

Henry had only ever been to one baseball game. Really he was not a man for sport at all, but when Fred came by in his new flatbed and blowed the horn, something in Henry jumped up before he even knew what it was.

"What's all this racket for?" Henry asked Fred.

Fred whispered as though his trip was a conspiracy, "Southeastern division! Delia beat the whole goddamn South. They're having a victory party at the river. Word is our Reds have that place taken over." Fred grinned. "Look in the back, Henry."

Henry lifted a flap of canvas to reveal several cases of beer. He quickly pulled the flap back, hoping the neighbors didn't see. His was a good Methodist neighborhood.

Ula Mae, Fred's sister, leaned over from the passenger side and said, "I heard they have champagne and a full band. You will dance, won't you, Henry?"

"Dance in the water?" Fred asked, cocking his hat back on his head. "It's a pool, not some joint."

"They're wild, they might. Remember when they started that big fight in Americus halfway through the eighth inning? The radio said it was utter chaos. You were listening, weren't you, Henry?" Ula Mae said.

Henry had been listening to the Carter Family on the Opry all evening.

"Come on Henry, let's go. You don't get out enough."

Henry got his clothes. On his way back way out, his mother asked, "Who is making such a racket in the drive?"

"Just an acquaintance. I shall not be long."

"Do not stay out too late, the bishop will be at service tomorrow."

"Yes ma'am."

Fred slapped the steering wheel when Henry squeezed in between him and Ula Mae. Soon the wide streets and well-kept lawns faded to woods and shotgun houses west of town.

"Feel around under the seat, Henry, see if you find anything," Fred said.

Henry bent and reached under the seat. There was a half-full half-pint jar. "That's the good stuff," Fred said, "some of Marlow's. Go on, try a sip." Henry flushed. He imagined his mother's and the bishop's scowls foregrounded against the church's white doorway.

"Well let me try it, if you won't," said Ula Mae, taking the jar. She took a dainty sip and then a longer one. Fred chuckled. "Old Marlow's whiskey will come up on you about like he would—sweet and smooth, but before you know it, you're face to face with an old swamp runner. And he don't let go easy."

"Oh Fred, hush," Ula Mae said, turning to Henry. "He always gets like that, every time I drink any little thing! He starts all this seduction talk."

"Just trying to protect your innocence, Uly," Fred said.

Ula Mae took another sip. "I don't know what innocence you think you have, what with that letter you sent to Gladys and all this whiskey in Daddy's new truck—which you borrowed without asking—and I don't even need to mention that woman on Coney road—"

"Woman, be silent!"

They hit a pothole and lurched, coming down in a flurry of elbows, shoulders, and half of old Marlow's liquor. Fred started to explain, "It was just a sappy old love letter Gladys held on to for no reason."

"She always was sentimental," Henry said.

"And Pa said I could take it out. I'll have to haul cotton in it anyway."

"It does take some practice to learn the gears," Henry said.

"Henry, don't take up for him like that," Ula Mae said.

"Do you want to swim across the river?" Fred asked.

"You wouldn't kick me out of a borrowed truck."

Fred and Ula Mae kept going until they came to the ferry landing. Bubba Evans came out of his shack. "One dollar, mister," he said, and Fred handed him a silver dollar. Bubba dragged the cable to pull them across the river.

Over the slosh of water, Henry heard dance music, shouting. Electric lights reflected in the ripples of the river. The pool was a beacon, bounded by shadowed water. "There is music, I told you there would be!" said Ula Mae.

The ferry slid up the bank and Fred drove off and parked by a bus. "The Reds' own bus, Henry!" he said, slapping the side of it.

They walked through the gate of the pool into a gold-lit world of noise. The water seethed with hairy-chested men and suited women. Arms lifted brown bottles of beer. A handful of musicians played Dixieland—Henry recognized Bissett on trombone and Leon on trumpet. Beyond them, he did not recognize half the people there. For all he knew, and it seemed so, half of Georgia was in that pool.

"Suit up, Henry," called Fred.

"I could not find mine," Henry said. In truth, he did not own one.

"Just jump in in your underwear." Many of the men and even a few of the women had done so. Henry felt out of place in his shirtsleeves and hat. A man in shorts bumped into him. "Have some hooch," the man said through a red forest of beard. Henry took the pint jar and sipped, thinking liquor might help him loosen up. Finding himself among such a rowdy crowd and already so much sin, he might as well drink. Fire with fire, sin with sin. The liquor burned but he made himself drink two good swigs before he handed it back to the man and thanked him.

Henry stripped to his shorts. He folded his clothes and placed them on a bench in a far corner, his hat set atop them. The pool was packed, man against woman, skin against skin. There was an unopened beer on the bench. Henry took it and slid into the pool.

Pushing through the wet mass of bodies, Henry searched for Fred and Ula Mae, or anybody he might know. Finding no one, he turned to a group of four men, one of them in a Reds baseball cap, and introduced himself. He told them he was from Delia and asked where they were from. They were all quite drunk, but Henry could not leave just after he had made introductions. One man said, "From Valdosta, all the way up here to celebrate."

"That ain't nothing, I came from Athens."

"The hell with Athens, I came from Ocala."

"What the hell you here from Ocala for?"

"To watch baseball, dumbass, why else?"

Henry was not sure if they were joking or about to fight.

He grabbed a passing liquor jar and took a deep few swigs. He left the baseball group and looked for women to talk to. Three of them stood sipping beer and he pushed through warm bodies to get to them.

Breaking into their circle, Henry saw Ula Mae. "Isn't it wild?" she said.

"Yes, it is," he said, but he was not sure if she heard him since they were adjacent to the band and Bissett had played a loud glissando. Ula Mae made swift introductions of which Henry remembered none. Then Ula Mae filled any possible silence with gossip about Fred and Gladys and how she jilted him or he jilted her. Henry was not sure which. He turned to one of the other girls and said, "Did you travel far to be here tonight?"

"What?"

"Where are you from?"

"My girlfriend and I came down from Vienna."

"I am from—" Henry began, but a trombone slide stuck into the space between them. The girl's eyes crossed looking at it, before it disappeared back the way it came.

"I need to find my friend," the girl said. "She always does something wild at parties like this. I have to keep an eye on her. It was good to meet you." And she pushed through bodies and was gone. Ula Mae still talked.

Henry tried vaguely to follow the girl. Hands clapped him on the back. He saw things terribly clearly when he looked directly at them. Everybody was golden in the electric lights. Others laughed and it made Henry laugh. His ideas against drink and debauchery rapidly changed. Still, he wanted to talk to a woman. Talk, and bring her over and sit by the fire, listening to the Opry. More than anything, he wanted some girl to call on, to take out. Henry had the handicap of shyness and the constraint of a zealous mother, not that those things should really be stopping him. Then and there, he vowed to relax his strenuous life and live like he imagined one of these revelers lived. At least in part. He took another drink.

By now he was used to the noise, sweat, men yelling and girls giggling, and him pushing his way among them, looking for that first girl he had talked to, or another one whom he could talk to. He heard a laugh like back-porch chimes, and turned. There was a woman laughing, her hair curled and untouched by the water, her skin the color of honey in the lights. Her eyes were dark, were as comfortable in this place, probably in any place, as Henry was apprehensive. He pushed towards her, focusing his failing concentration on her, until Fred grabbed him by the arm.

Fred leaned against the pool edge, smoking a cigar. "Did you hear what she said?" Fred asked.

"She only laughed; I was trying to—"

"Ula Mae's told everyone from here to Carolina about Gladys, inventing half of it and blowing the other half up big as the moon. She's even spilling out every terrible rumor that's gone around about . . . Coney Road . . . you didn't hear her?"

"She was," Henry belched, "talking."

Fred turned a frightening shade of red and struck the water and called Ula Mae a name that Henry would never repeat.

"She can walk back to town then—swim! I'll pay Bubba not to let her back on the ferry. She can't just go and tell all about that—Hell, she's Gladys' friend too, they go to goddamn Sunday school together," Fred said. He grabbed his hat, shoving it into Henry's chest as he spoke. "This is the way they are, these women, Henry: nothing but mouths with pretty legs. She's jealous of Gladys, I'll tell you, she can't stand a girl with pretty blond hair like that. She'd tear it all out if she could and laugh. What do you think, can't you see it? Can't you tell it about her?"

Henry took a jar from beside Fred and drank a long swallow of whiskey. Fred stopped him, his eyed wide and focused toward the diving board. Henry turned. The woman he saw before stood there, nude, bathed in the dull light. All the water stilled and all the rowdy cries ceased. She stood like a goddess carved in honey-colored stone, as though polished marble held all the delicate curves along her hips, or else she was a tongue of flame solidified, swelling and tapering. Her face was unashamed, bearing a small smile not of drunk wildness but of quiet uncruel mischief. In that gleaming sliver of time, she looked at Henry in a way that bathed light into every part of him; not desire, nor lust, but a warmth that would remain forever, smoldering, wakened to flame every now and then or dying down, but never extinguished. Henry watched every sinew in her frame shift as she dove, disappearing without a splash into the water, her feet kicking up like a last burst of fire. He barely heard the hoots and jeers as she swam the length of the pool and rose on the other side, where the woman from Vienna covered her with a towel. She blew a kiss and faded beyond the water and people and debauchery and extinguished from sight.

Fred didn't speak. Henry pushed through the bodies. Shoved through them, he realized, but it was not from anger, so he did not say "Pardon me" as he had the whole night.

He passed Ula Mae, who said "Henry have you seen Fred?"

Henry said, "Yes, and you should avoid it."

Bissett's slide blocked him for a moment and he pushed it back, making an off-key slur that Bissett worked into the song anyhow.

Henry passed the baseball men from Valdosta and Athens and Ocala. They yelled gibberish. Henry gently pushed one aside like a door and pushed him back after he had passed through.

Finally, Henry climbed out of the pool. The red-bearded man was still sitting on the bench with a jar of whiskey. Henry said, "Where did that girl go?"

"Girl?"

"The one from the diving board."

"How'd she dive through so many people?"

"Sheer beauty. You didn't see her? She swam through and came out right here."

"Have some hooch."

Around the edge of the pool there were only couples, or drunks sleeping, or the shining brass of the band.

Outside the sounds were muted. A large moon hung and flickered in the sloshing of the river. No one was out there. Henry would have called out, but he never learned either of their names.

On the ride home, Fred said through clenched teeth, "Uly, I told you not to talk any more about me and Gladys. It ain't nothing to talk about."

"Who told you that? I didn't say a single word except the bald facts of it."

"Bullshit. You were blabbing about it to everybody! What's going to happen when she hears about it?"

"For one thing, she'll be glad she didn't end up with a bastard like you."

"Woman! Take that back, or God so help me—"

"Fred, shut your damned mouth," said Henry. Ula Mae and Fred stared at him, jaws slack. Henry continued, "I'm sick of hearing you two. All this hatefulness turns my stomach."

Fred mumbled. Ula Mae sighed. They didn't speak any more on the way to take Henry home.

The next day, Henry woke up late and told his mother he would not be attending services that day.

"But Henry, the bishop will be there."

"A bishop isn't that special. I'll go next time he stops by."

He drove out to the river and went to get his hat from where he'd forgotten it on the bench. Henry tried to picture the woman on the diving board again, and he felt, lighter within him, that same warmth he felt when she looked at him. But by then she wasn't a thing for picturing. He crossed the ferry and headed towards Vienna.

Snakewater

Mark followed Pen across the clay-colored road, carrying a bass rig and his father's tackle box. The old shack's paint had long peeled and its tin roof glowed a dull unreflective red in the summer heat. The boys stood for a moment frozen before it. Then Pen climbed the bowed front steps as though approaching an altar and set a bottle of whiskey on the porch. He backed down the same way. No one came out to receive it. Pen motioned for Mark to follow him down a trail beside the house. They didn't speak until they were out of sight of the low-slung shack, where no one might look out the windows and see them.

"There's his still," Pen said, pointing to a chimneyed lean-to.

"You can see it from the road. Won't he get caught?"

"Pap Marlow don't give a damn." They both looked back when they said his name.

The trail to the river went down a steep hill. Old man Marlow had tied ski-rope, baling twine and seat belts in switchbacks along it. It all looked like streamers in the trees as they approached. Pen tromped down, his hand loose on the lines. Mark scuttled sideways, hoping the trail didn't give way and send him, fishhooks and all, falling into the Flint River. Pine and rough hickory shadowed the river, along with the vines that ran along them all, nearly blocking out the sun. At the bottom was a wide brown sandbar by a calm stretch of water. Pen looked south, toward where the lake widened, studying the water for strikes. He looked north, upstream, where the swamp choked together on either side. "We'll go this way," he said. Mark peered along the sandy banks. Going north looked like going into the jungle.

"Wouldn't it be easier to go downstream?"

"Yep. But if we go far enough, we'll be in everybody else's fishing spots. Upstream, we're going to fishing holes nobody but Marlow drops a line in."

Shifting their gear, the boys walked up the bank, keeping to the sandbar as much as they could. Mark watched for alligators.

Brush and redbug moss hung over a coarse sliver of sand where dull water lapped. Their tennis shoes sloshed in the mud, soaking. All the surface was still. Every now and then Pen's head jerked up to catch a strike in the distance. Mark concentrated more on his steps and watching for water moccasins.

"How old is Pap Marlow?" Mark asked.

"How old? You might as well ask how old the river is. How old that stump there is. Some folks say he fought in the Civil War, then came back and took a Creek wife. That he cooked gator tails for General Lee. I've heard that he was a knife-thrower in the circus until they kicked him out." Pen paused. Mark knew this trick: Pen was luring him into continuing the tale.

"Why'd they kick him out?"

"Well, he was in love with one of the horseback riding girls, prettiest girl in the whole circus. But she didn't want nothing to do with him and told him so. She said, 'You're a bore, Marlow! I thought you would be a good man, but you're just like a nasty little child!' So he got piss drunk the next night, called her up to be his assistant for the knife-throwing act and chucked a Bowie through her heart." He held a thorn vine back so Mark could pass. "He's still got that Bowie with her blood on it. Carries it with him everywhere he goes."

"You don't know that. You ain't seen him."

"Well Joel's cousin's older brother saw him one time playing poker at Camper's Haven, said somebody tried to cheat him and that knife hit the table red as an apple."

"He saw it?"

"Plain as day."

Mark said, "He won't come after us, will he?"

"Only if you keep talking so loud."

Perry sat with his feet propped on the steering wheel of his tractor and rolled a cigarette. He watched his mule grazing.

It was getting late in the summer, fading fast to August. Tall grass waved beneath pecan trees and that was all the noise there was. It was ten years since Perry got off that ship, eleven since a kamikaze buzzed the control tower so close Perry saw his teeth. Years of cattle and orchards, tractors and combines, raising a boy. It didn't seem like all that long.

Perry swabbed a handkerchief across his forehead. The pecan orchard looked clean and ordered. Even the old dumb mule seemed content. Perry got into his truck and pulled out to the road.

Some godawful crooner played on the radio, but the windows were down and he couldn't hear it well anyway. Halfway back to the highway bridge, Perry saw Will sitting by the side of the road in his old straw hat. There was a bony dog beside him. Perry pulled to the shoulder. "You drunk?" he asked. Will unfolded his limbs and stood.

"No sir, just need a ride to town."

"Where'd you find that dog?"

"He found me. His name is Tramp. He's got gas something awful."

Perry chuckled. "Put him in the bed and get in."

They crossed the bridge with Will holding his hat on his knee and Tramp's ears flapping. "I saw your boy walking with Oscar's boy down by Camper's Haven," Will said. "Looked like they were going fishing."

"Reckon where they were headed?"

"They go much farther up there, ain't nothing but Marlow's land."

"They ought to know better than—" Perry broke off as a smell wafted into the cab. At first he though he'd left some fertilizer in the bed but he owned none quite so pungent. "Did he shit back there?" Perry covered his mouth and nose with his forearm.

"No, sir. He's just got gas something terrible."

Perry gunned the accelerator. Looking in the rearview, he saw the dog lolling his tongue like somebody had pulled his finger.

Will said, "He just walked up to me. He's a sooner type. Sooner one as another."

Perry pulled off at Oscar's store. It was a little clapboard two-room deal with gas pumps outside. Will followed him through the door. Tramp sat panting in the truck bed.

Oscar, Perry's brother, had the same godawful crooner playing on the store radio. "Morning Perry. You getting Will a drink?"

"No sir, I'm off the likker," Will said.

"Suit yourself," Oscar replied, and took a swig of gin.

"The boys tell you where they're going today?" Perry asked.

"Yep, Boy Scout slough."

"Then why'd Will see them up by Camper's Haven?"

"It looked like they were going fishing," Will said.

"There ain't nothing up there but Marlow's property."

"Nothing at all. And there's no telling what Marlow'd do to trespassers."

"They know that. We didn't raise fools."

"We raised boys. They ain't far off."

"That's a point, there." Perry paced in the small store.

"I heard you got to give Pap Marlow some likker if you go by there. Folks that don't leave him some likker float up later with knives in their backs," Will said. "But then, I also heard he's got goat legs under his overalls, which I find difficult to imagine."

"And he's got a water moccasin for a dick, from where a witch cursed him," Oscar said.

"And I bet he shits turpentine." Perry ran a hand over the sweat continually beading on his forehead. "Oscar, are you coming or not?"

"Yeah. Let me get a few things."

"God, Oscar."

Oscar went to his stockroom and rummaged around. "Per," he said, "I'm missing some whiskey." He came back with a clear bottle and some pork rinds.

"The boys come by here today?"

"Yeah, early."

Perry said, "We'll go find them."

Mark couldn't hear the road anymore and the water was so still it didn't make any noise. The August swarm hummed in the trees. Already sweat soaked his back and gnats flew around his eyes. Pen walked out onto a fallen cypress and scanned ahead. "We got to cross the river. You willing to swim?"

"Ain't there water moccasins and alligators and snapping turtles?"

"Yeah. We'll find a shallow place."

Pen took off his shoes and knotted the laces and held them with his rod and tackle box above his head as he stepped into the river. First it came to his knees, then waist, then neck. Pen wavered in the middle but stood firm, longways with the current. Plodding, he made it.

Mark took off his own shoes. He held them above his head. "Come on," Pen said, "You want Marlow to catch up with us? We can't be out here all day." Mark waded in. Warm slime on the bottom gripped his foot. Step by step, like Pen, he went until river water nearly lapped into his mouth. He closed his eyes and felt the cooler undercurrent help lift his upstream foot. It felt like yards upon yards before the water grew shallow and he emerged with Pen on the other side.

His cousin slapped him on the shoulder. "See, you could make it. No gators."

Mark walked along the edge of the clearing. He stopped over a white mass of bones laid on tufts of gray fur as though arranged on a carpet. The ribs lay in barely crooked sequence and the long skull's toothiness made him uneasy. His father had cleaned deer, but Mark had never run across a skeleton just left somewhere. The empty eye-holes seemed worse than the pink flesh appearing from the whispers of his father's skinning knife. Even the way the blood drained into the old washtub was not as odd to him as the thing curled in a soft pile of its own former skin.

Mark shuddered and jogged to catch up with Pen. "Ain't we about to the spot?"

"Getting there."

They walked back to the bank, Mark looking back every now and then.

"So when are you going to ask Lexy out?" Pen asked.

Mark felt his already hot face redden. An image of the freckled girl pulling sandy hair behind her ears made even the swampy, sweat-soaked river disappear for a moment. He glanced at Pen. "Soon, I guess."

"You better. How long you two been passing notes and talking every day after class? Ain't you tried to kiss her yet?"

"Kiss her? Shoot, Pen, I—"

"She'd know you liked her if you'd kiss her."

"But you can't just walk up and kiss a girl."

"If you know how to do it right. Sweep her off her feet."

"How am I supposed to sweep a girl off her feet waiting for the bus after school?"

"Don't you know some poetry or something? Out of all that mess you read all the time?"

"How far to the fishing spot?" Mark asked Pen.

"Little ways, to where the river narrows. We're getting there."

Perry leaned half out the driver's window, Will folded himself into the middle with his hat on his knees, and Oscar, slap-drunk at noon, wedged into the passenger side, the arm holding his gin cocked on the window. Tramp sat in the truck bed, panting.

"Perry, you know them boys are fine. They take guns?"

"Why would they take guns fishing?"

"Why the hell not? Might need them for alligators, snakes—"

"I don't let Mark carry a rifle off by himself."

"Pen keeps one by his goddamn bed. They can handle them."

"I know." Perry considered explaining his ideas of responsibility to Oscar, but it probably wouldn't do much good. He breathed out. "We'll go and find them, and if they've gone onto Marlow's land like a pair of damn fools—" the thought turned his spine cold despite the heat—"Then we'll talk to him. Something."

Another waft of the dog's fart came in through the windows. This one smelled less like fertilizer and more like an opossum who'd died under a piece of steel roof in August.

"God-son-of-a-bitch-damn," Oscar said, and stuck his head out of the window as though the passing air could wash out his lungs. Oscar yelled a few more things that no one could understand over the wind.

"My apologies Mister Oscar, he's got gas something terrible," Will said.

"How did that stink even get in the cab?"

Oscar looked back. Tramp wagged his tail. It banged once against the steel bed.

Perry sped. Dust dry from a week without rain whirled around the truck and into the cab. Perry and Oscar had been to see old Marlow before, back when they were young men before the war. He remembered the old man's sprawling beard, the narrow slit-eyes of the kid.

Oscar coughed from the dust. "Jesus Perry, is the devil behind us?"

"We got to get out there before they get on his land—"

"What?" The crunching sand of the road drowned out anything but yells. Orange grit moved over everything in the cab. Will pulled a handkerchief over his mouth and Oscar coughed like his guts were coming up. The last betrayal of the mutt formed as a thick vapor and assaulted all three of them.

"Son-of-a-goddamn-bitch," Oscar said. He doubled over and raised up like some demon was coming out of him, then spewed a thick spray all over the truck, inside and out. It pooled in the upturned brim of Will's hat and splattered on the windshield. Unable to see, Perry hit something large with the truck, bumping over it. He slammed on the brakes.

Perry looked at Will and Oscar. Will dabbed stray vomit from his shirt with the handkerchief. Oscar groaned with his head against the dash.

"You all right?" Perry asked.

"I'm going to kill that dog," said Oscar.

They pushed open the doors. Perry walked around behind the car and swore. Oscar came and stood beside him.

"That's Walt Jessup's mule. Or was," Oscar said. The animal lay with two lines of tire tread across it. It didn't look surprised, but none of the men could remember a mule ever looking surprised. "Now you owe a man a mule." He thought he could make out the imprint of the Chevy logo on the mule's side. "Maybe he'll take Gertrude, like a trade."

Will walked to them. "Tramp run off. Is that Mister Jessup's mule?" he said.

"Was," said Oscar.

Perry shook his head and turned. "Come on, let's go."

Oscar said, "Reckon why a mule was just sitting in the middle of everything?"

"We got to find the boys. you jackass, get in the truck!"

Hitting or driving over the mule had thrown something off in the truck and it felt shaky. Perry made Oscar clean the windshield with a rag and drove somewhere between 30 and 35. The men spread out as wide as the cab allowed so they wouldn't have to smell one another.

The narrow aisle of the river fork became darkness the further Mark and Pen went into it. Ropes of briar hung over the thinning sand bar. Mark wondered how even the tiny swamp deer made it through to water. The stream carried shafts of light up from its depths which waved together like a cloudy gem turned one way and another.

"I should've brought my gun," Pen said. He held his small fishing knife before him like a saber.

"Papa told me I couldn't bring mine without him."

Pen crouched like Indians in the movies. Mark saw the swamp on either side of the branch as a black wall. He imagined it breathing as he breathed.

Their steps became careful. One rock to another, one sandy patch between washed-up mussel shells to another. Everything slowed and the deep noises under the the trees grew. Every moment Mark fought an urge to run wild back through the stickers and past the cabin and right up Marlow's hill. He couldn't let Pen see such cowardice in him.

The branch was only a dozen yards wide, maybe less, and shallow.

Pen held up his hand. His shoulders tensed with breath.

A length of ridges undulated downstream, long as a johnboat. The black sharp depths of eyes rose from the water giving way to a prehistoric snarl of a head, its jaws lined with white jags of teeth. It crawled toward them. Pen backed into Mark, brandishing the feeble filet knife to the iron skull.

Oscar had thrown up once more, completely out the window this time, and a few strands of it hung from his beard. "How much farther?" He asked.

"Til we get there."

"I reckon we'll have some tea on Marlow's front porch. I'm sure he's got some all mixed up, waiting for company."

"We didn't bring no likker to give him," Will said. "Folks are supposed to bring him some likker, or else he scalps them and uses their hair to make fishing lures."

"You still got that gin, Oscar?"

"Shut up before I hurl."

Perry's gut clenched. He thought over all the bloody stories of Marlow the elder and the younger, and of those two dumbass boys traipsing out to the boonies to fish. Pen might've known better but probably ignored the knowledge. Mark—if the boy survived, he was going to get a hell of a whooping later. Perry remembered taking Mark fishing on the pond at the orchard.

"That's the house yonder," said Will. They got out and stood at the foot of the porch. Perry stepped onto the groaning boards. He looked down to be sure they were stable, and when he looked up it he faced a wild-eyed grin framed in a dark gray beard. Old Marlow stood with a red cleaver of a knife. "What are y'all doing up this way?" he asked, not three feet from Perry. He remembered seeing tracer shells fly over the flight deck, but they were dull compared to the sickle-sharp blade held toward his ribs.

Mark and Pen backpedaled. The alligator moved toward them not with animal motion but inevitability.

A shot barked. The side of the gator's head popped. It jerked, jaws still wide, and then lowered to the sand. Mark and Pen panted. They looked to the other bank and saw nothing. A voice proceeded from it, "What are you doing in my waters?"

The man emerged shirtless and every cord of his muscles twitched. He held a rawhide-laced rifle. His eyes shone with pupils so tiny the whole eye seemed nothing but gray and white, the eyes of a night-creature. They locked with those of the boys and seemed not to see them directly but saw them whole. The knowledge behind them, like a deep, cold cavern, must have been terrible; a knowledge of sharpness and cruelty and death. The boys cowered before him.

He waded through the river holding the rifle above it. "It would've eat you and shit you out upriver. You see that?"

They could do nothing but nod.

"Why the hell you on my waters? The old man say you could?"

Pen spoke, drawing all his strength he could. "We left him whiskey. That's the deal."

Marlow the younger cackled. "Cause he ain't got enough?" He was not tall, but there was more of him, a density. "What was you go'n do when that gator come up to you?" he said to Pen. "Stick her with that pocketknife? You came up here with nothing. And you," he turned his gaze on Mark, "Get out from behind your brother. Be a man." Mark felt that the space out from behind Pen was groundless. He took a step, and another. He faced the alligator hunter full on.

"You cast a line?" Marlow asked.

"No sir. We were trying to find a good hole," Pen said.

"You think I fish up here?" They looked at him. "You see me with a pole? I eat the snakes and gators, I eat the things that try to eat me. My old man taught me how to hunt and how to die. It ain't a big thing once you can see it, but once you do then you can pull death's tongue right out his mouth. You boys know how to die?"

They shook their heads. Marlow glared at them with a terrible grin, then drew a knife and held it out by the blade to Mark. "Take it," he said. "And slit that gator's throat. See what it's like."

Mark looked from the rough blade to the huge dead alligator. He didn't want to see Marlow's face. His whole body buzzed as though one stray splash or noise or word would send him running whether he wanted to or not. Breathing deep, he took one step toward the scaly corpse, then another. With each step he imagined the head rising again and grabbing him and tearing him apart. Its black eyes looked no different dead than they had alive. Mark knelt beside the alligator and lifted its massive head. Marlow pointed, "There under her jaw, boy. All the way across." Mark filled his chest with the stench of stagnant river and shoved the knife up to its hand guard into the scales. Half-looking, half-thinking, he sawed it across to the other side. The flesh peeled like paper. Redness gushed and swept down the bank to darken the water. Marlow took the knife back and pierced the boys with his glare. "Now you know. A little bit anyway," he said. With one wrench, he turned the monster on its back and opened its body and threw organs out from it into the river. He reached in to his shoulder, yanking out lungs, liver, heart. Marlow bit into the raw and steaming heart. They watched him chew and swallow the meat before he turned and said, "You boys pick it up. You're gonna carry it back home." He strode down the sandbar.

Pen picked up the tail first, keeping his hands well away from the flaps of hanging hide. Mark, already blooded, hooked his fingers through the throat, his arms around the head. It was still warm. The boys thought it would drown them by its weight.

They followed Marlow back downriver, stumbling. Pen dropped the tail once and Mark hissed at him to pick it up before the hunter saw. Mark's own fingers and arms ached, but they didn't shake any more. He felt wet with blood to his elbows, smeared with it like with axle grease after helping his Dad fix the tractor.

At the bottom of the rope-strewn hill, Marlow stopped. Sunlight streamed in through the branches and everything waved in the breeze. "The house is on up yonder. Leave it here. Don't come down here no more, and if you do bring a damn gun next time." Then he moved into the darkness below the open treeline and was gone.

The boys dropped the alligator and fell beside it. Everything was quiet and Mark noticed it for the first time. Just wind. Trees. "You all right, Pen?" he asked.

"Yeah." As if awakening from a daze, Pen studied the tackle box flung over his shoulder. "We didn't ever get to cast."

Perry assumed that this was it: time to get stabbed by a crazy swamp whiskey runner and die. He thought about Virginia back at home, about Mark. Would he go to college, or stay in Delia working the orchard? The thoughts flew: how would the boy remember him?

Perry looked into Old Marlow's booze-addled eyes, narrowed toward him, but they shifted. First a glance to something behind Perry, then a full gaze, then a sort of chuckle. Perry turned his head, keeping one eye on the knife and stretching the other to see what the old man was looking at. Will stood with a drawn revolver aimed steadily at Old Marlow. "I apologize that we came to your property without any likker to give you, Mister Marlow. However, I would appreciate it if you wouldn't point that knife at my friend like that. He only came up here to make sure his boys were okay," said Will.

Old Marlow laughed and stuck the knife in the wood siding behind him. "A man can't argue with that. Y'all want to come in for a sip?"

Oscar coughed and climbed the steps. He paused for a moment beside Perry, turned to see where the revolver was pointed, which was nowhere since Will had put it back wherever he kept it, and went on inside. The old man laughed and clapped him on the back.

Perry felt like his asshole was up in his stomach. He let out a long breath. "Thank you," he wheezed, "Thank you, Will."

"Yes sir. Things would've been easier if we would've brought him some likker to begin with."

"Likker to begin with."

The men sat in ragged cane-bottom chairs, passing a jar of clear liquid. Shaken as Perry was, he stood in awe of Old Marlow's moonshine. If half the stories were true it could fuel a car, cure polio, double as perfume, and kill vampires. He pulled up a chair and once the jar came to him he took a small sip, then a larger one. It burned then tasted like nothing but sweetness once he got it down. He passed the jar to Will, who held it for a while and passed it back to Old Marlow. Oscar was telling the story of the day. "Then I said to myself, 'That's Walt Jessup's mule,' but 'was' was more like it." Old Marlow roared with laughter at the terrible things that had happened to them. The sight of that beard opening in joyous sound put the others at ease.

The whiskey began working on Perry, as well as a desire to keep Marlow happy, and he told a story. "I was watching my mule this morning," Perry said. "There was a goose following him around digging all the corn out of his manure like they do. Every stack of turds, that goose dug through it like it was starved. Then I see that mule's tail swishing, and every other swish shows something bright on his rear end. The mule had one kernel of corn stuck right on top of his asshole, right at the crown—and the goose saw it too. He comes creeping up behind, wobbles his head a little bit thinking he's actually going to grab the thing. Then right when old mule's got his asshole stuck out as far as it'll go, that goose jumps and shoves his bill right up there and the mule spooks and sucks his asshole in and that goose is up to its neck in the hind end of him. My mule bucked around the field with a white goose flapping out of his ass. Finally he ran off, or they did, and it looked like my mule had grown another fat tail. No telling where he shit him back out again."

Perry watched the men double over and took another sip before passing the liquor.

There came a howl from outside. The men leaned sideways and Perry spun to look out the front windows. "Look, Tramp's found us," Will said.

"Will," said Oscar, "Give me that pistol."

"Rosie! Get in here," yelled Old Marlow.

"Rosie?" asked Oscar. "That's your dog? And you named her Rosie?"

"She's a fine coon hound. Named her after a woman in Memphis." Marlow scratched the dog. "She gets the shits when I feed her leftover corn mash."

Marlow looked with quick sobriety, if not a menace, at Perry. "You say your boy came up here?"

Perry felt caught in that snake-charmer gaze. "Yes sir, they came up here this morning to fish. I was going to go find them before they got on your land—"

"And mine," said Oscar. He belched.

Marlow released his gaze, nodded. "My son's out hunting, he probably kept an eye on them." Perry didn't know if that was reassurance or a threat. His guts knotted as he pictured the younger Marlow's cold eyes again. "Would you mind if I went and looked for them? I'll go along the river quick as I can, just to make sure they didn't meet any trouble."

"Go on." Old Marlow drank.

"I'll go with you," said Will.

Perry moved faster down the hill across the ropes than his feet could keep up with. He slipped every other step and Will grabbed his arm and helped him up. The whole trail was slick with mud.

At the bottom, Perry ran to Mark. The boys sat in the mud and leaves of the bank, covered in blood. "Son," Perry shouted, gaining all the traction he could in the clay, racing to where Mark sat. Another image of reddened bodies flashed in his mind—red fire and red blood after Zeroes had strafed the deck. Perry held Mark's face, didn't see death in his eyes. Then he felt his son's arms, chest, legs.

Mark said, "The blood ain't ours. It's from that," and he pointed to the carcass of the alligator.

"What the hell—you boys all right?"

"Yes sir," they said together. Dirt caked their shoes, and their arms were dark with blood. Their faces were streaked with grime and small cuts like they'd run through thorns. Neither boy smiled. No injuries.

Perry opened his mouth to holler at them, tell them just how much trouble they were in, but he saw something in their faces. Mark was scared because Perry was scared, that made sense. But Mark also had a look of understanding. Perry had told him stories about the war, but they were boisterous as the newsreels they used to watch in the briefing room. Seeing the teeth of kamikazes and all that. Somehow Perry knew the time had come for the real stories. The ones about ocean storms and the devil-flash of incoming machine guns—about death.

Perry grabbed both of them in a big embrace, one knee on the pebbles of the bank. "Come on, boys. Y'all hungry? We'll clean you up and get some lunch."

"Camper's Haven ain't far," Will said.

They walked back to the road and Oscar joined them from where he sat on the porch. He had wedged a pint jar in the hip pocket of his overalls. "Jesus, Penner, is that blood from you?"

"Naw, from this gator we killed."

"Oh," said Oscar, and he took a drink.

For the first time in his life, Mark saw his father as another person, not some omnipotent figure. The fear on Perry's face had shaken him before he realized it was the same fear he'd felt seeing the alligator crawl toward them. Whole conversations formed in his mind, talks for hours between the two of them, but he didn't know the questions to ask nor how to initiate them. Perry, for his part, looked forward to sitting and eating in a familiar place, watching his son bite into fried catfish. Oscar talked with Pen, telling him about Rosie and the mule and Will's revolver.

Mark told Perry about it a few times, but never the whole story. He told him about going to fish. He told his father about the alligator because he was proud of it. But whenever Mark told it, Marlow cut the throat, making that dark blood run into the river. It was a hard story to tell sitting around the living room, as though it could only exist where that dark water slouched through its Channel, opening into the lake where all things became bright and diluted. Mark never learned that, try as he might, neither could Perry dredge up all the stories he needed to tell.

Songs on the Water

The bucket truck ahead of them rumbled down the rough asphalt in a halo of the rising sun, those beams breaking from the raised support posts and splitting into rays in the windshield. Mac drove—one, arm across the wide wheel. Dale leaned his head back on the plastic seat-top. Both men took intermittent sips from their first Styrofoam cups of coffee of the day.

"I'm going to kill him," Dale said.

"No, you ain't."

Deperro broke through on the CB. "Did you say Hatley or Old Hatley?" he asked.

Mac picked up the spiral-corded mic. "Left up here, like I told you," he said. "It's Old Hatley."

"Maybe not kill him. Maim him."

"It wouldn't help."

"It would sure ease my mind."

"You're the one that wanted him there."

"Nobody ever wanted him anywhere. I wanted lower rent; I didn't count on living with the biggest asshole in the county. How can you stand him?" And then, "And why are you sticking up for him?"

Mac picked up his coffee cup with his fingertips. There was not a sure way to explain how he stood Randy. He hadn't figured out for himself how those chords he heard coming across the slough could be from the same faith as could produce Reverend Randy Sneidel.

"Because I have more patience than you, I suppose," Mac said.

"That might be true. He didn't run off your girlfriend though, either. Don't you get tired of all the church talk? I've been to church and all, but there comes a limit."

"He's the wrong kind, is the problem. Weird beliefs."

"You got another girlfriend?" Deperro said over the radio.

Dale glared at the speaker as though he could glare at Deperro through it. "You been listening this whole time?" Dale asked the air.

"The mic's on."

The two men looked, and the mic was wedged between Mac's leg and the seat, pressing the transmit button down. Mac chuckled. Dale did not.

"You could've said something," Dale said.

"I did."

"About the mic."

"But it was interesting. I thought you had broke up with that girl. What was her name, Angela?"

"I did."

"Back together?"

"No. This is a new lady friend."

"You go through them like socks, Dale."

Like socks? Dale mouthed at Mac. Mac shrugged and turned up his lip. "You two just drive."

"Cain't but one of us at a time though."

"You know what I mean." Dale shoved the mic back in its holder. He picked it up again. "And stop being a smartass," Dale said, tossing the mic to the seat. He wiped the side of his face.

Mac thought back to Sunday morning the day before, sitting on his dock waiting for the boat church to begin. Pontoon boats, speedboats, and little fishing trollers rode out to a spot close to the bank of the lake, forming their own rows for worship. Mac only saw them headed that way, he couldn't see the actual gathering. But if the wind was right, Mac could hear them singing four-part harmonies. The sound pulled him from his world of sweat, grease, and loneliness into one that felt higher and seemed more proper to what it should be. Mac didn't believe, necessarily, but the music was a thing past belief. Or it didn't ask him to believe, only to listen. The voices began soft, growing stronger as they settled into the song:

Come thou fount of every blessing,

Tune my heart to sing thy grace

Streams of mercy, never ceasing,

Call for songs of loudest praise.

The verse came mixed from quarters, each harmony guiding itself by another and clasping themselves together. No part stuck out, nor did a single member of that informal choir weaken the sound by fearing to sing. Mac had never heard anything like it. The song became a wondrous unity; a living, breathing, moving thing unto itself. The voices widened and deepened and climbed:

Teach me some melodious sonnet,

Sung by flaming tongues above.

Praise the mount! I'm fixed upon it,

Mount of thy redeeming love.

The song reached from the dawning sky to the dark murky depths. When it touched the water, the water resounded and added itself to the song. When it touched the far banks where eagles nested and alligators rolled, it thundered back upon itself. When it soared through the trees, it touched each and was by each touched. The voices multiplied and grew and expanded. They became a substance of unity. They surrounded him, and became part of the world in every direction around him.

Mac didn't always know what the words meant, not being religious, but when he heard the people sing, he found himself in a different world, one meant to be beautiful. And that made sense enough.

That was before Randy moved in with them.

"We should have known," Dale said.

"What's that?"

"The minute we saw him come in with that Bible. Thing looked like a beaten dog. He didn't look much better."

"I think we did know. I did anyway."

"You could have filled me in."

"I'm not sure if you were as perceptive about the whole situation."

"And those little Civil War men. What did you make of them?"

"Everybody's got a hobby. That might have been the more normal of the man's interests."

"Damn things were probably made out of lead."

"Which do you think he liked less," Mac asked, "Those bottles you left out or the number column?"

"Oh, definitely the column. I wouldn't be surprised if he calls all those poor girls, preaching to them. But I still wish you wouldn't call it that."

"It's a column full of numbers. So what else am I going to call it? Your phone book? Most folks use a book, you know that?"

Ahead the bucket truck turned and for a moment the side of Will's face was in its own halo of sun until pines broke it behind him and Dale followed through the turn. The truck's transmission upshifted with a burst of smoke. Already the morning sun had heated the day.

"What was it he said," Mac asked, "About God giving him a place to stay?"

"Something like that. God is cruel if such was the case."

"Could be your moment of testing, Dale."

"I dropped out a long time ago."

Deperro on the CB: "Y'all talking about that roommate still? Same one that called Dale at work that time?"

"Jesus, don't remind—"

"—That was funny as hell. Was it your nudie posters he found?"

Dale cussed under his breath.

"I mean, I know you're a supervisor and all, but I ain't heard cussing like that since my Daddy—remember he was in the navy—came back, and you know that gonorrhea can show up months after you—"

"Gonorrhea. Now that'd be a good thing for Randy to get," Dale said to himself.

"Dale, ease up now."

"Maybe the witch'll give it to him."

Mac snorted. "He didn't have anything going on with her."

"I told you what I saw," Dale said.

"What'd you see?" Deperro asked. "Don't be keeping secrets."

"Cause you sure don't; your Daddy must be—"

Mac took the mic and said, "Dale came home unexpectedly one day and found the good Reverend in an uncompromising situation," Mac said. "But I think he's exaggerating the situation."

"That so? And this was the witch, right?" Deperro asked.

"The same," Dale said. "I came in and she was standing outside our front door, peering into it and the look on her face suggested confusion, revulsion, maybe a desire to vomit. I round the bend to see why, and it's because that hound has his shirt off and appears to be pleading for something or other."

Silence for a minute until Deperro came back with a voice shrill from laughing, Will's deeper voice in the background. "And you don't think he had any luck?"

"Surely not after that," Dale said. "That was the only time in my life I've preached, and I can see the appeal of it."

"I hope for her sake Mabby ain't got nothing to do with him," Mac said. "She's got more sense than that."

"You know her?"

"I talked to her at Big John's a few times. Most folks are too scared to talk to her."

"She deserves the world, if only for giving me the satisfaction of catching the bastard with his pants down. Or near about."

They drove between fields of white cotton blooms under spraying bowbacked sprinklers. A single streak of cloud—like a brush stroke—spread from one horizon to the other. Mac generally tried not to hate people, not out of moral conviction but because he knew what that anger was like, and he'd spent enough time in it following his divorce. His life had the rhythm of a paid profession and a few good friends to drink with. No lack except for loneliness when he thought about her. Even then, he didn't trust his memory of things, the idea of it he had constructed. So he grew a beard, bought a record player for all his old Merle records, and stopped hating.

"There's only the one thing that really gets me," Mac said.

"Only one?"

"Eileen."

Dale shook his head and sighed at the travesty. "Shoot. I thought she'd fight him."

"He deserved it."

"I know which way my bet would have gone."

Dale considered Mac's answer. Finally, he said, "Why was that one so bad for you?"

"It was just awful."

"Yeah, it was. But why'd that bother you more than everything else?"

Mac considered. "It has to do with me having some sensible idea of everything."

"All right."

"Because Eileen, she had just invited us to that boat church."

"Knowing we wouldn't go."

"But she invited us anyhow. Sipping on whatever that cheap beer is that she drinks. And she's such a decent woman. Then you got Randy, getting all upset because of the bottle. The woman just did something kind and good, something you'd call Christian, and Randy couldn't see past the bottle."

"Mm-hmm."

"It's night and day. One of them has sense. The other's so worried he can't take a step without worrying whether it's sinful. I don't know how to take the thing overall."

"The thing."

"Faith. God. Meaning of the Universe. I don't know."

Dale picked up a socket wrench and sat playing with it, turning the ratchet. Finally, he said, "Maybe the thing is just broke. Maybe it doesn't make sense."

"There's got to be more to it than that."

"There ain't. Eileen has sense; Randy doesn't. They just happen to be people of faith on top of that."

"That's not what I mean."

"Then what do you mean? This is a hell of a conversation for Monday morning."

The bucket truck pulled over to the grassy shoulder and lined up its crane with the telephone pole where they would replace the transformer. Will and Deperro climbed down and opened compartments on the sides of the truck, drawing out harnesses, long rubber gloves, and hard hats. Mac and Dale pulled on hard hats and there in the silence were four men still in clean shirts with dew under their workboots. There was a silence over the fields and the scrub pine woods that made Mac feel heavy, rooted—dug into the land. Will and Deperro rode the bucket up, their canvas toolbags swaying against the side.

"Will, you're getting this one," Dale said.

"But you said I could get the next one."

"No, Dep, I said when you stopped acting like a fool once you got up there you could get one."

"But you promised."

"No."

"When the hell did I act a fool?"

"When you bent that cradle trying to bang it out with the side of your wrench," said Will, who mimicked the act with his tongue out and his eyes crossed.

"Y'all ain't funny."

"You know what ain't funny? Insurance hikes coming out of my paycheck."

"The deductible only went—"

"Let Will do it."

Mac listened. Evidently, Dale would oversee the job, so he only looked over the lines and named each piece of hardware in his head. The grounds, the cradles, the various half-inch bolts. Leafy vines obscured one of them, glowing green in the morning light. "Are those Southern lines above ours?" He asked.

The men looked. "Yep," Dale said. "Reckon we need to radio back and check on them?"

"Amy said they were clear."

"Would she know?"

"Should. She's the one looking at the display."

"We'll be cautious." Dale yelled to Will and Deperro, "Can y'all two be cautious?"

"Day and night."

Dale sighed and scratched his head. Mac watched him—watched his hands behind him against the pickup's hood. Often Mac tried to replicate Dale's ease, his calm way in the world. As though loneliness happened only to some people. They were both past middle age, and Mac felt anything but wizened by his time. As long as they'd known each other, he could not tell if Dale took stock of his own wisdom. Maybe it didn't occur to him at all.

Mac asked him once why Dale stopped going to church. The first answer had something to do with a woman, the second with war and pain and violence.

"When I was a child," Dale had said, "I went to church every time the doors were open. I read my Bible every night and had four silver dollars I got for memorizing Bible verses, knowing 'Jesus wept' didn't count. All that was bright and made sense when I was little, when I thought my Daddy could do no wrong and Momma would make sweet rolls every morning of my life. Even as a young man, I generally stuck to it if I didn't feel too bad for running around the way I did." Then Dale summed up the rest of his life with a shake of his head and a swig of beer. "There comes a point," he said, "Where all that stuff doesn't hold up. Some things you see that nobody should have to see. Things that nobody should have to deal with. I yelled at God before, wanting him to yell right back. Then I just kept on living."

"You couldn't pick it up again? Figure out a way to reconcile those things?"

"Not if I was honest with myself. Maybe when I'm an old man."

"Eileen goes. I've heard her read the Scripture at that boat church."

"Well."

"It still works for her."

"It's a woman's thing anyhow."

"That's a cop-out."

"No, it ain't. Go to any church you want, count the men and women, see how—"

"That's not what I mean."

"What then?"

They'd been smoking on the dock, tossing cigarette butts into a tin bucket. Mac said, "I thought you liked feminine environments."

"To a point."

Dale's gaze did not waver from the men in the bucket. Mac looked up at them and trusted Will's slow movements, his constant gaze at the transformer connections while they hooked up the crane. His eyes did not move when he reached back for another tool from Deperro. The men were silent, and all the sound around them was the running diesel engine and the soft clatter of tools on bolts. Then there was a shift and the transformer leaned forward into Will's arms like a tired child. Its wires bowed from the line, and Will settled it on his shoulder and the edge of the bucket. Mac could see him breathe; his movements were so deliberate. All was still in the risen July sun and his mind as he studied it, only a snatch of song lighting the back recesses. Then a loud crack, a mechanical groaning, and Dale screamed.

Mac turned. Two lines flailed, crackling in the air. The bucket rocked and Will fell. His arm hit the ground before he did. Dale ran to him. Mac ran to the truck, grabbed the box behind the seat, and poured antiseptic onto Will. Blood pumped through the charred places in bursts. Dale tightened a tourniquet with a wrench tied up in it. Mac poured the alcohol, concentrating there and not on Will's face. The man jerked. He didn't wince at the antiseptics. Mac didn't know if he was even still alive—but he must be if the blood pumped—and Dale dug in the kit, his Army training working between his cussing.

"Get Deperro," Dale told him.

Mac touched Will's shoulder. He felt full of air, like his guts had all fallen out, and his mind couldn't do anything but follow the order. When he rose to get Deperro, Will's warm blood was on his hand.

"Deperro," Mac yelled. The bucket looked empty. "Oh God," he said. Mac searched the ground to see if he had fallen as well. Then a hardhat poked out of the bucket.

"Did they shut out?"

Limp lines. "Yeah, they shut out," Mac said.

"Did they get Will?"

Warm blood on his hand. That blackened smell. "They did. You all right?"

"I'm coming down."

Mac saw the bucket work, ran to the cab, called for an ambulance on channel 9 and called Amy on the company channel. His voice was high and fast when he told everything both times. They assured him they were coming, and he sat back. For a moment, he couldn't move. He hollered out to Dale.

"You call it in?" Dale said.

"Yeah."

"Then just pray."

Mac looked and Dale was bloodied on his arms and across his shirt. Deperro knelt, his hand on Will's shoulder, whispering to him, maybe telling him the same dirty jokes they dropped playing spades. Trying to laugh Will back to life.

Mac might have prayed. His heart drummed, and he couldn't get enough breath. Was Will going to die? Had they witnessed his death? Time passed, and all Mac remembered was holding his hands together, the palm with drying blood against the clean one, until he didn't know which was which.

When they got home they sat in the truck before they walked in. After going to the hospital, the office to explain everything, and the gas station to buy cigarettes. Mac and Dale were quiet, staring at the house. Mac said, "You think—"

"Do I think he'll make it?"

"Yeah. Make it."

Dale lit and blew. "The man lost a lot of blood. With his heart problems too—but they can reattach arms, you know that? Bone, veins, nerves, everything. I've seen it."

"Over there, you saw it?"

"No. Saw it on the news."

They sat. Mac said, still in some ripple of shock, "Did you see anyone die over there?"

Dale didn't answer for a while. He never talked about the war and Mac had learned not to ask about it. But Dale said, "Yeah. I saw people die."

"I haven't. Not until today, if . . . " Mac trailed off. The possibility hung in his mind like every piece of bad luck in the world wrapped into one.

When those cigarettes were down to the filter, Mac and Dale walked inside with some weariness, knowing Randy was there and not wanting to deal with him.

They went in and ignored Randy. Dale cracked open a beer. Mac looked at the beer, got one himself, and lit a cigarette even though they'd agreed not to smoke inside. They sat on the couch and didn't say anything. Randy stood in the corner and began his usual beratement. He said, "You two drink when you're lonesome."

"Ain't lonesome."

"Then depressed."

"You could say that."

"If you drink when you suffer, you'll never be sober."

"Why would we want that."

Randy shook his head. Something in how quiet they were must have clued him that this wasn't a normal day. Maybe he recognized that something was wrong. He asked them what it was.

"Had an accident at work today. Might have lost a man," Mac said.

Randy's gaze fell. He stood with folded hands a minute, perhaps in reverence. "I'm sorry to hear that," he said.

Randy watched them while the men stared at nothing. They had showered at work and changed clothes, but Dale still had dark stuff under his nails.

"I'm sorry," Randy said again. "I hope that he was right with the Lord, that he's with God now."

"He ain't dead," Dale said.

"Oh. I'm sorry, the way you said it—"

"Give it a rest, Randy."

"What are you saying anyway?" Dale said. He raised his head and glared at Randy.

Randy raised his hands in deference. "Only that I hope he's fine. I'm sure he'll be fine." Randy should have stopped but couldn't. "But only that Heaven and Hell are realities, and I certainly hope your friend—"

"Will. The man's name is Will. His wife is named Vivian and they have two kids, DJ and Chloe."

"I hope Will has accepted Jesus into his heart or that God has mercy."

Dale crossed the room and lifted Randy by his shirt front. Mac called after him. Dale said to Randy, "You sure as hell won't talk about Will like that."

"Dale."

"If you say another word about him, you little twerp, I'll take you to that lake and I'll hold you under until you drown." Dale dropped him and Randy crumbled against the wall. Dale stormed out to the dock.

Randy lay there, his shirt disheveled. His mouth opened and closed. Mac stood over him, fury flowing into and out of pity so that he didn't know whether he wanted to beat the hell out of Randy or apologize to him. Finally, he told the preacher, "You ought to go. Be out of here by Monday."

Randy spoke without looking at him. "I didn't mean—"

"You said it anyway." Then, trying to be kinder: "It's best if you leave."

Randy nodded, his chin falling into his shirt, his eyes wet and bewildered. He said, "I know. But I didn't mean to say about your friend, about Will—"

"This is your problem, you always got to have something else to say. Why can't you let things be sometimes?" Mac's fists clenched. He left Randy there before his anger got the better of him. He walked to the dock and sat with Dale. Their cane poles jutted against the reflections of stars and a heavy moon emerging from the pale cloudless sunset. Ripples lapped against their dock and against the knobby roots of cypresses.

"I told him to leave by Monday."

"If he's got sense he'll go tonight."

They drank. Mac was tired from hours of waiting at the hospital. He thought about the possibility that such a stark belief as Randy held might be the reality of the world. That heaven and hell were things he ought to be worried about. Then he dismissed that thought. He didn't want to hold onto faith out of fear, if he ever got that far. But Mac wanted to hold on to something. He looked at Dale's beer.

"Dale," he said.

"Yeah?"

"We should go to the boat church."

"That is not my current inclination. So no."

"It just came into my head."

"Put it out then." Dale drank. "If I needed any more evidence of how little I need all that church mess I just saw it."

"They wouldn't be like him."

"They wouldn't be all that different."

"Eileen ain't like him."

"Of course not." Dale turned to face him. "It's not the people; it's the whole idea of it. I'm not going to go pray to a God that lets good men have their arm burned off and then lets someone talk about how they deserved it—"

"He's full of shit. And he didn't say that."

"Might as well have." Dale sat back. Mac knew Dale was even more exhausted than he. Dale said, "You mean God or Randy's full of shit?"

"Randy. Yes, Randy, dammit."

"Well." Dale drank. "He gets everything he says out of the book. And the worst part is, I remember reading the parts he talks about. It doesn't bring me hope. Hell, it does the opposite. Ain't that what it's supposed to do, bring people hope?"

Mac didn't answer.

"What makes you want to go all the sudden?" Dale asked. "Feeling a need to flee from hell?"

A need to flee, a need to return. Wouldn't he want one as soon as he had the other? As terribly sure as Randy was, Mac wasn't afraid of where he would go when he died. If it was pain, he knew what that was like, having had Will bleeding at his feet and not knowing what to do about it. Mac said, "What happened today, that could happen to you or me. I don't want to hold back doing something, especially because of that little bastard in there." He gestured toward the house. "I feel like that boat church is a good thing, and I want to go while I've got the chance. That's all."

"And you want me to go too."

"Just so I ain't by myself."

Dale watched him. "A good thing, you said."

"Yeah."

Dale fumbled with his beer can for many minutes. Finally, they heard Randy's car crank and pull away. The old contraption backfired. After its noise had disappeared down the road, Dale said. "I'll go. Once."

"Would it help to bring a few beers?"

"Can you?"

"It doesn't seem to bother Eileen."

"Then yes. I will go with you to church so I can drink." And Dale drank.

It took some cleaning Sunday morning for Dale and Mac's bass troller to look presentable. There had been a mayfly hatch and hundreds of dead insects clung all over it. Once they brushed it off and stocked the cooler, they cranked the little motor and idled out of the pinch. They passed the IDLE ONLY buoys and pushed the throttle, soon finding the small congregation of boats.

There were perhaps twenty in all. They came up next to Eileen's pontoon boat and tied theirs to its railings. She smiled. "Good to see you boys," she said.

Mac tipped his Power Company hat. Dale raised his beer and looked around to see if anyone had seen it.

They had a standard welcome and a few announcements. Dale tried to open his beer as quietly as he could. Somebody said a prayer, and the men took off their hats. When the priest announced the hymn, Eileen leaned over her pontoon boat's railing to hand them a hymnal. She laughed as they crowded together to read it.

Every time Mac had heard these hymns, he had been off in the slough, the sound dulled by trees and distance. Now, at the source of the song, it was a controlled, soft thunder. Voices all around them partook. He became lost in the parts as they layered one upon another and flowed through one another. He heard all the additional and deep sounds: the song rolling across the water and rebounding back across the lake. He heard it strike the pines and cypresses on the bank, echoing with a woody quality. His recollections of the hymns heard on his dock were shadows of the song he heard now in the midst of its singers.

Here I raise mine Ebenezer;

Hither by thy help I'm come;

And I hope, by thy good pleasure,

Safely to arrive at home.

The verse rose and its sound drowned the memory of Dale's anger. Mac remembered Becky smiling instead of shouting, and for a moment—a fleeting, brief moment—he believed deeply that Will would be all right. Mac saw Will's face was not pinched with pain, but halfway through the worst joke he could tell, laughing. All of them sit around their plastic lunch table, playing spades and laughing.

Mac thought of Randy, and finally felt he could forgive the man.

The song ended. Mac sat and the sunlight felt good on his shoulders.

Dale drank five beers during the sermon. He kept shaking his head and by the end just looked at his feet.

Eileen waved goodbye to them afterward and everyone went on their way. "It was good to see y'all," she said.

"So what'd you think?" Mac asked as they moored the boat.

"It was about what I'd expected."

They went later to visit Will at the hospital. He was slow, and weak, but he grinned up at them, and pointed to his arm all wrapped in bandages. That afternoon Mac watched the sun fall blazing into the lake. He listened to the water, and the creatures, and heard Dale whistle a phrase of hymn.

Idle Only

James woke up with the covers all off him, the box fan blowing in the window and Mabby asleep beside him. Her thick hair tangled over her face and the pillow. He slid out of bed, stretched and pulled on his robe to go make coffee.

It was probably nine o'clock, judging from the cool slanted sunlight and the quiet of everybody being gone to work. The coffee maker gurgled. James watched the calm lake waters a while until a loud outboard engine buzzed the silence all out of balance. He walked down the backyard to the dock. Sure enough, it was Alvin in his old buoy-boat. Hailing him from the dock, James leaned over the rail and set two mugs down on it.

"Morning, Gillespie," Alvin yelled, mooring.

"Morning, Sergeant. Coffee?" James said. Alvin only called James by his last name, and James only called Alvin, Sergeant, because of jokes they had made one drunken night at Big John's.

"Sure, thank you." Alvin, a sun-soaked and tattooed old man, looked James over. "You forget to get dressed?" James looked down at his robe and bare legs. Alvin wore battered jeans and a frayed shirt, like always.

"No, not so much that. I forget why Mabby's in my bed again this morning."

"I doubt that. The forgetting, anyway." Alvin leaned in toward James. "You know she's a witch, right? Cursing a man if he looks at her funny?"

"Aren't they all witches, Sarge?" James sipped his coffee and saw a heron glide over the pinch.

Alvin glanced up at the house, as though he might see her in the window. "You better watch it. If you piss her off, no telling what might happen to you."

"She'll turn me into a frog?"

"How many toes she got?"

"I'm not really into that kind of thing."

"Well." Alvin spat over the side of his boat. "Just watch your ass, Gillespie. Thanks for the coffee."

James accepted his thanks and watched the little steel boat, loaded with buoys, idle back to the channel. Then, walking back up the yard, he saw Mabby in the sliding glass door. She was wearing one of his shirts. The sun caught her green eyes.

"How's that old salt, sugar?"

James looked at her feet. They were strong, dusty like always, ten toes gripping the threshold. "I'm going to work for a little while. You can watch the TV if you'd like," he told her.

"I won't." She smiled her dreamy smile, and went to his small bookshelf. James sat at his desk and turned on his computer and monitor. He set a graphing calculator and a small slide rule beside a notebook detailed with figures. James worked online for the next hour or so, managing his stocks and some emails about his rental properties. As soon as he had returned from Kuwait, he had put some of his earnings in the stock market, traded, and began to suspect that he was uncommonly good at foreseeing changes, at knowing outcomes. He had checked every finance and economic book out of the tiny Delia library. James invested in real estate, or at least some cheap houses and duplexes. Within a year, he was living comfortably on his returns, plus a little more from some online advertising ventures. James worked several hours a day, managing everything, but never more than a morning by then. Beyond that, he possessed an abundance of daylight hours to spend as he pleased.

Mabby came and coiled her arms around his shoulders. James flipped off the monitor.

"Let's take the boat out, Jimmy. It's a gorgeous day," Mabby said. She pressed her head against his, with no hesitation or holding back. James wondered if somehow Mabby knew what was coming. If she did, it did not change her.

She helped him uncover the speedboat, then lay along the bow in her swimsuit. James saw the three small moles on her belly, the ones he could find without looking. He put on a pair of sunglasses and idled past the buoys. Alvin had scrawled on one, "Watch Ur Ass!" Mabby saw it.

"Your friend Alvin must've wrote that. What did he tell you to watch your ass for?" she asked.

"You," James said and smirked.

"He doesn't even know me," she said. Mabby watched the buoy pass and lay back on the bow seat.

Noon sun crushed over them, as though its weight was what kept the water flat and serene. Behind his boat, that calmness tore into a narrow wake. James opened a beer and drank from it. They rode along the populated side, toward where the houses grew large and ornate with thick Greek columns and several back decks, swimming pools and hot tubs. He pulled close to the bank and idled past. Every backyard was immaculate: the pine straw in the beds was deep brown without a hint of gray, there were no leaves or pine cones in the yard, nor toys nor any odd vehicle parked. New brick, light red and clean, rose unbroken for three stories. The window curtains all matched and the wood-slat blinds were half-drawn, a balance of privacy and exhibition of the fine furniture inside. James knew that those rooms would be furnished with stained wicker loveseats, oak bookcases and TV stands, a few issues of Southern Living spread nicely on the coffee table. Woven palm leaf ceiling fans, spinning quietly.

Mabby, the wind no longer snapping her hair around, looked out across the lake. After laying the cool glass against her neck and chest for a while, she opened her own beer. "Can't we get going, sugar? These are just old rich people's houses."

"I want to see if anyone's moved into the Tudor."

"The what?"

"This one." He cut the engine alongside a lofty house of stone and dark, thick beams. Its windows were diamond-paned, with small crests in stained glass. The backyard, mostly bare beyond the back deck, was like a territory unto itself.

A woman in chocolate-brown slacks and a sleeveless blouse walked onto the back deck. She moved so lightly that the stone mansion behind her looked foolish. Lifting a hand against the sun, she looked out to the lake.

James watched her every move. He threw off his sunglasses and stood squinting to see her until she turned, without a sound, and went back inside.

Mabby held the beer against her neck again. "I guess they're moving in. Were you thinking about buying that huge thing?" She looked at him and saw that he still watched after the woman from the mansion. "Sugar. Jimmy," she said. He turned, looking toward her. Yes, that sorrow in her eyes. "Jimmy, let's just go to Big John's and get lunch."

He did not respond, but started the motor and pulled into the channel.

The marina was a low shack with a wide wood dock, gray with age, and dead mayflies hung in all the corners. Big John, who slathered pulled pork onto sandwiches for them, was a dense mule of a man, with a long and surprisingly clean gray beard. James and Mabby ate among old men gone fishing and young men with wave runners. They drank sweating beers in silence, until Mabby, without looking up, said, "Where have you gone, Jimmy?"

"I haven't moved at all."

"That isn't what I mean."

They spoke quietly as the bar patrons clinked glasses and laughed around them.

Mabby said, "I know things change, I know that people change. But, maybe I didn't think you would."

"My aims have changed, but nothing else."

"Aims?" Mabby looked at him. "I suppose so. They've been changing. And now that woman is one of them."

James was silent.

"If you don't want me any more—hell, want. I never wanted you to want me." She drank. "I will still love you, after I've hated you for a while. Maybe these 'aims' will make you like yourself again, but I don't know what was wrong with things. You're being an ass." Mabby stood and took a few dollars from her pocket for Big John. She touched James on his shoulder, and he didn't turn around. But he felt it, as she meant for him to. Mabby left walking toward the bridge.

James finished his beer at the marina and then went to the resort lounge across the lake for a martini. He walked into the new, shining bar in his khaki shorts and a half-buttoned linen shirt, both wrinkled from where he threw them on that morning. He ordered a dry Beefeater and wondered how long it would take the new bartender to realize the drink was his usual.

Not long before, loosened by the gin, he began asking the other patrons if they knew who was moving into the Tudor. Finally, a stout woman with symmetrically short hair answered. "Her and her husband bought that house. He's some big lawyer in Albany and they wanted to get out of the city. I don't think they have any kids. He's only got one arm."

"What is her name, do you know?"

"He's Mike Eleazer. Don't know what her name is."

This answer did not help him. He knew the husband's name would be disgusting and he cringed thinking that the woman must bear it, have it cover over her own name. He asked, "Do you know what she does?"

"I know what she doesn't do, and that's work. Hubby makes enough that she stays home, or goes shopping, or whatever the hell she wants." She peered through caked mascara at James. "She's taken, mister. You may have to look elsewhere," she said, leaning towards him and waiting for the next curve in the conversation. James placed a ten and a five on the bar and left.

Piloting the boat back to his house, he saw dark banks of cloud a few miles beyond either side of the lake, each pouring silent rain like pale silk. By the time he pulled under his boathouse and got inside, daylight was gone from gold-blue to a weak bruised gray, and the shadows hazy and tumid. James sat in his screened-in porch and heard the first droplets pelt his steel roof. It was a dull noise that calmed all the lake noise of outboard engines, passing planes, and geese. In his little world, he watched all of nature become soaked through; the pine trees turned black and slick, his boathouse boards darkened as with stain. He could not remember what it was like with Mabby even the night before. It was as useless as trying to remember exactly what the coffee had tasted like that morning. He recalled only the look of her freckled back, uncovered, and her hair flung around her head. She was the sheets, all scattered, twisted, and sweat-soaked. A darting memory of his early time back, of he and Mabby dancing at Big John's in a haze of redneck tunes and beer, came and was pushed aside. Then he thought of the woman in the Tudor: how lithe her limbs, how full of grace.

James stood and walked through a misting sheet of rain to the boathouse and started the boat. It had no canopy and rain stung his eyes as he pushed the throttle as far forward as he dared. Cutting a wide arc outside the slough, he bounded over the wind-driven waves several dozen yards from the bank, passing the houses and mansions that glowed from within in the storm.

The Tudor loomed, near black against the sky. A dull amber light was far back in it like a candle at a wake. James stood soaked and watched and waited and did not know whether to plod wet up to the back door and demand to see her, or to yell from his boat, or to just give it up. He did yell, just a bark that slipped out, but it was drowned in the rain. He did give up, but his rebel hands did not start the engine again to leave.

He was steeling himself to go the door when Alvin, inexplicable in the buoy-boat, pulled up beside him. "Looks haunted," said Alvin. "You ain't thinking about buying that one, are you?"

"I will buy it."

"What's wrong with the house you got?"

"She—"

"She? Who's she?" Alvin watched him a moment as James mouthed words and stared at the house. "Oh, I see. Now I see." Alvin took a bucket and absent-mindedly bailed rainwater out of his boat. His wide canopy kept everything except his feet dry, and he propped those on a cooler. "Gillespie," he began, "I told you. I told you so several times in fact. Did you see the buoy?"

"I saw the buoy."

"You saw the damn buoy. And still, what did you do? You went and pissed off a witch and now you have ceased to be the smart, calculated fella you were and have become a soaking-wet fool, hollering in the middle of a rain storm. It didn't even take a day."

"It wasn't like that. There's no hocus-pocus and you know I don't believe in that anyway. Sergeant, have you seen her?"

"Not since then, she probably went home."

"No, the woman who lives there," James said, throwing his hands toward the house.

Alvin looked up at the house, which he'd never paid attention to before, then to James. "I'm beginning to suspect your butter done slid off your biscuit, old boy, cursed or not."

They were the only boats on the lake, two bits of flotsam in the whole wide water. Black waves wobbled them, clanking the steel gunwale against the fiberglass. James said, "I drove a truck over there, Sergeant. There were bullet-proof screens and Bradleys in the convoy, and there were days when the guns would ring out or an RPG would fly past my windshield every few hours. They had me hauling gasoline. When I wasn't terrified, when I could think, you know what I thought about?"

"Women?"

"I thought about how I never wanted to work like that again. They paid me well, but you can't pay me enough to ride a firecracker through hell like that again."

"All right. That explains why you sold the rig when you came back."

"I had plans for a big house, a corvette, a new speedboat. Any number of things that fit my paycheck like a glove. The figure was big, especially when I looked at it all at once. The glamour of it took me over. I thought up thing after thing, each one more shiny and meaningless than the one before it. Eventually, I thought of insurance and luxury taxes and upkeep, but that was already after the long parade of toys had slowed and soured to me.

"I knew I couldn't blow it all away like that if I wanted a new life. So I saved, scrimped, bought that dump of a place in the slough. I hit my stride on the stocks and still, I kept my hand

close. If you knew how much I have saved—if you could imagine the liquid assets I have, ready to buy and furnish any house
on this row—I've got the mind to do it, Sarge, to put myself in a
place like this," James said, "With such a woman as that."

"You've certainly got the mind," said Alvin, "I don't doubt
that one bit. You've got a dozen times the mind I've got. You had
mind enough to quit working and then mind enough to pull a
trick where you got some cash without doing hardly nothing.
Had mind enough to rent out shitty houses all over town. That's
mind and will, to be able to do all those things." He spat tobacco
juice into the rain. "But I'm beginning to think the witch had
precious little to do with your current foolishness. Hell, not
even the woman in that house had to do with it."

"Mabby's not cursing anyone. She knew what she was getting into. It's not my fault if she expected more from me. With
this woman, whoever she is without that damned husband, it
will be different."

"It ain't about the women. What you've gone and done,
Gillespie, all by yourself and only to yourself, is you've tied your
own carrot to your own stick and shoved it up your ass." Alvin
stood, rocking his skiff. "You were happy when you moved into
that dump in the slough, and you were real damn happy when
you found out you were done working and you could make
hundred dollar bills fly off the computer and into your lap. Now
you've got your sights set on a bigger dump and a woman you've
never met nor seen more than once. It doesn't make a bit of
sense to me."

"I could buy it any day. Any moment."

"And you'll be tired of it the next day."

"Within three months, there will be a new car in the drive-way. Within six, one for her, and a new boat within a year. New clothes. She won't have to work or do anything but be beautiful and let me keep her."

"One or both of those ain't going to last long."

"And I'll forget that other shack, and Big John with all his rednecks. I'll leave behind all this hick grime I've been stuck in my whole damned life."

"Well." Alvin said. He leaned against his console. "Maybe you can do all that. Seems like you'd be better off just drinking some beer and fooling around like everybody else."

"No. I need more than that, Sarge."

The outboard engine bucked to life. "Then so long from the hick grime, tycoon." Alvin wiped his hands together and raised them to James in dismissal or exasperation, and piloted his boat away toward the dam.

Ten months later, James had the house. Not only the house, but a German car in the driveway and all the rooms stocked with furniture and a huge heavy roll-top for his computer. A full-range stove. Polished granite shower. King-sized bed.

It was quiet that night and he walked down his footlighted backyard to the dock. Gentle ripples beat his boat against its moorings in rhythm. He looked out across the lake to the other side where a single dock light glowed before a newer mansion. Hands at his sides, he gazed at the far-off brilliance of it for a long while.

He noticed a buoy bobbing twenty yards out from his dock. It read "IDLE ONLY." James raised a revolver and shot it five times, the crisp slap of the reports skimming across the water. The buoy rocked, but it didn't sink.

The First Thing You Lose

That night I looked up from *The Dark is Rising* to see my cousin Branhan walk in with a faded cowboy hat in his hand. His boots clomped on the hardwood floor. Aunt Rose talked and talked along with my other aunts Kathy and Mary Lynn. I listened but somehow all that talking held nothing for me. Branhan stood with his hands in his pockets. I only saw him every few years, when the aunts visited and brought him along. Maybe it had been three years. That night was the first time I really looked at him. "What're you reading?" he asked, turning to me. I showed him the worn cover. It was from the school library. He nodded, smiled, and looked away. I couldn't tell if he was young or old.

That night we ate fried steak, potatoes, and squash while Aunt Rose asked Branhan all about his new job at the paper mill in the town where he lived. I kept quiet as the long minutes ticked by. Finally I was excused. Listening to the grown-ups exhausted me.

The next morning Branhan sat outside in a plastic chair, a cup of coffee steaming on the porch's floor beside him. Aunt Rose had gone earlier to Perpetual Adoration at church, where she prays or sits in the chapel by herself for an hour. It was about the only time my Aunt got to be alone. I ate my biscuits and preserves in near-silence, by myself as well. Once I finished, I eased out onto the porch. Branhan's face seemed quiet, if that makes sense. Not just on that morning, but always. I remembered his sad smile from the night before and realized he had felt as exhausted as I had. He looked younger, too, in the still morning, as though he wasn't all the way an adult. Branhan said, "Mornin, Alden."

"Hi," I said, and sat in a chair a few feet away. I didn't really know what to ask him about but he didn't seem to be in any hurry to talk. He wasn't like other grown-ups in that way.

"You sleep good?"

"Yessir."

"You ain't got to 'sir' me, it's all right."

"Okay."

"After Uncle Haig's show, I was wondering if you two would go with me to the farmer's market."

"Uncle usually goes on Sundays anyway."

Branhan nodded. Birds flapped up under the porch to their nest above the light fixture. "School going all right for you?" Branhan asked.

"It's fine. Are you—" I wasn't sure at all—"Are you still in school?"

"Oh, no. I'm working. We got the horses to look after too."

"Y'all still have horses?"

"Twenty of them. Four of them are ours, the rest are boarders. Really it's too many on six acres." Branhan lifted his cup and held it in both hands. "Do you ride, Alden?"

"Only that one time at y'all's place. Back when—" I froze, wondering how to say what I wanted to say.

"Before your aunt passed away," he said.

I didn't say anything. When I peeked at his face, Branhan only watched the line of pine trees in our back yard.

After a while Branhan sipped his coffee and said, "Merlin. That was the horse you rode when you were there. He's a retired racer."

Uncle Haig hollered outside when he was ready. His voice was never quiet, even when he whispered, and his yell was always too loud. He had on his overalls and a red cap to celebrate the Bulldogs beating Tennessee. We piled into the old truck, me shoved in between Branhan and my uncle. Branhan rolled his window down and watched the road ahead like an old dog. "You should've kept watching the game, Al," Uncle Haig said, "They done whooped em. Just straight whooped em!" I nodded and fiddled with the radio.

We got to the farmer's market and parked in the dirt lot. It was a sort of complex, with livestock pens, some food vendors, a small produce, and flea market. We walked to the main building, where a sign advertised "Wild Mustangs, $30 and up." Uncle Haig went off to talk to some of his friends, probably to kid one of them about the game since he wore a UT cap from time to time. I went to the chicken coops.

My rooster was there—black and white, no red on him except his comb. He remembered me every week when I came with Uncle Haig. Collecting a few pieces of dried corn from the ground, I held them out. My rooster came to eat them from my hand. Branhan hunkered beside me. His clothes smelled faintly of leather and new sweat.

"You got a way with animals," he said.

"This guy knows me." We stooped there, me feeding my rooster and Branhan handing me pieces of corn and feed scattered outside the cage. I suppose I should have felt strange having him there, since I didn't see him that often, but he was easy to have around. His jeans were frayed at the side stitching and his boot heels were worn white.

It was something about sadness. Not many people in my family seemed to understand how sad people need quiet to be happy. The rest of them drank at every reunion like my parents and Branhan's dad didn't exist. Like there wasn't anything to it.

My rooster took a few more pecks at my hand and trotted off. We rose and walked past a booth selling quart jars of honey and another selling sweating glass bottles of milk, unpasteurized. More tables sold tools, knockoff shoes, fishing gear. Around the larger pens we heard a commotion: the snorting of horses and shouts of people trying to contain them. We leaned against a rusty pen section to watch.

Twenty or more horses eddied in the main arena. They called to one another. Men walked back and forth with lead ropes and halters, wrestling horses' heads and dragging them out to a trailer. The process didn't look fun for the men nor the horses. I saw a man jump back from a horse's kick. "They're having a hard time, aren't they?" I asked Branhan.

He nodded. Dust from the pens fell over us and gritted into my clothes. "You see a good one?" Branhan asked. I looked, trying to distinguish between one mottled coat and the next. I didn't know much about horses but I saw a rearing head, all white with a blue eye, wild and confident. I pointed the horse out to Branhan and said, "He would be a good one. Tough, though."

Branhan looked across to other enclosures. "Reckon they're using that round pen?" he asked.

"I don't think so," I said, but Branhan was paying attention to the horses.

After a while I got bored and walked on. I went to the food shack and bought a hot dog and some sweet tea. People walked by me in overalls, most of them fat.

By the time I got back, Branhan was in the round pen with the blue-eyed one. He had a length of rope in one hand and his back to the horse. It trotted back and forth, looking at him. Energy still twitched in its neck, in the way it bobbed its head. I watched for fifteen minutes or so, as the horse slowly calmed and nosed dry manure in the pen. Branhan stood, coiling and uncoiling the rope, not speaking. The horse crept closer to him, straining its neck to sniff more of his scent. Branhan didn't move or turn around. I was glad he wasn't kicked and trampled but I wondered what he was thinking.

Walking down the concrete aisle, I looked for Uncle Haig. I had an idea where he would be, but I didn't want to go. If he was there I could ask how much longer until we left. I pushed the crooked door open and peered inside. The room was utterly dark at first until my eyes adjusted. I scuffed my feet on a rough concrete step going down. Men filled the space and the smell of them filled it too. There was cigarette smoke, and finally I saw Uncle Haig's red cap jerking back and forth.

Men yelled and cussed, spraying spit and tobacco juice. They had just put in the next round of cocks and I stood on tip-toes to get a look at them. The first flew up: crimson with iridescent black feathers in its tail. They had gaffs on it. The cock squawked and hopped after the other one. Once I was close enough I saw that the second cock in the arena was mine, the black and white. He ran from the crimson—he didn't fight at all, just tried to get away. The men cussed and threw cigarette butts and spat tobacco juice that stained his feathers. The crimson pounced him again and again. Blood flecked the sand, darker than the crimson, more red than the tobacco spit soaking into sand. My black and white stumbled, flapped its wings, danced at the edge of the arena. He tried to jump out, but one man slapped him. My rooster moved more and more slowly, until the man who had thrown them in at the start climbed in and grabbed him. Half the men booed and the rest cheered. I saw Uncle Haig rubbing his hands together the way he did when he was excited.

I followed the man who held my rooster. Outside he dropped him in the dust. I went over and started wiping off all the grime. It stained my hands. My rooster's small chest rose and fell quickly and his eyes blinked. He wasn't moving his head. I asked the man if he thought my rooster would be okay. The man looked at me and walked back into the shed. I tried to hold the places where my rooster bled. After a while his breathing became more shallow. Finally his eyes stopped blinking. His chest still felt taut, still had its weight. I held my rooster to me and cupped his head where it lolled.

People bury dogs and cats. But, I wondered, does anybody bury roosters?

I picked him up and walked to the edge of the woods behind the farmer's market. There was already a small path, maybe made by deer, and big rock steppingstones across the branch there. It was late afternoon by then and the lowering sun lit up the leaves. Patting down a tuft of long, soft grass, I lay my rooster there between two pecan trees whose limbs hung down and cooled us. Warm wind whirled the boughs, a sound apart from the distant bustle of the farmer's market.

They say the first part of childhood you lose is that sense of no-time, when each moment is a long dream. The brilliant sunlight also dims, or escapes your notice. I walked back.

At the pen, Branhan moved in circles, clucking his teeth or saying "whoa." The blue-eyed horse moved back and forth. Branhan held the loose rope in one hand, barely raising it. I saw other men loading their purchases into trailers, pushing and shoving, dragging on lead ropes and slapping rumps to get the animals to move. A few horses reared. One man sat on an old tire and nursed some wound he'd received on his arm.

Booths closed down. People packed up their boxes of goods. Trucks and new SUV's glided past on the highway. I thought about those families, happy in their new things, going home to a normal life without glass doorknobs, drafty windows, tub baths—back to parents. I envied those kids, whose homes were filled with many good things.

Uncle Haig came up behind me. "What's your cousin doing?"

I didn't look at him. I didn't want to look at him.

Branhan turned in the center and the horse ran around him at the rail. "You ready?" shouted Uncle Haig. "You two go on," Branhan said, "I'll be there after while."

Uncle Haig looked around and seemed to grasp what was happening at the pens. "Did you buy that horse?"

"Yessir, I did."

"Son, we ain't got a trailer. How were you planning on getting him back?"

"I can ride her."

Uncle Haig laughed, a sound like a grunt. "You go'n ride your horse back along the highway?"

"Yessir."

"Cars and everything? Hell. Son, you got your horse-riding license with you?"

Branhan didn't respond. Uncle Haig made a soft, incredulous sound. Branhan did not move out of the pen, he didn't even pause in what he was doing with the horse. There was a tension and energy to his body that hadn't been there, or a power that had previously been muted. Uncle Haig shrugged and we got in the truck.

At home, Aunt Rose had left a few pimento cheese sandwiches on a platter under plastic wrap and gone to her book club. She would come back giddy with the wine they drank. I lay on my bed, trying to read, but ended up just looking at the ceiling and the long crack in it.

I don't know how long I was asleep before I heard hoof falls on the gravel drive. The horse blew and Branhan muttered something to it. I ran downstairs. Sure enough, there was Branhan astride the mustang. He sat bareback and used an old rope laced through the halter for reins. He stopped me by holding his hand up, and slipped off the animal's side. "Real slow and gentle, Alden, she's green." I nodded and inched forward, pushing the screen door aside. The horse was smaller than it had looked in the pen. I could look straight over her shoulder. She shook her head from side to side. Muscles hung and twitched on her chest. "That's it, Alden, gentle. Let her smell your hand." I almost jerked back when that heavy head turned towards me and saw me with its bright blue eyes. She stretched to sniff me, nostrils opening wide. Her breath was warm and smelled warm. "Pet her real easy on the nose. You're doing fine." It felt soft. Her lips smacked. Branhan smiled. He handed me the reins and said, "Just hold them loose, don't pull." He went to shut the gate. "I hope Aunt Rose don't mind if I let her gaze in the yard for the night. I hope she don't shit—crap in the yard."

"How did you do that?" I asked. "How did you tame her that quick?"

Branhan wiped sweat from her neck with the flat of his hand. He said, "It's all about listening. That's all it is."

He didn't say anything more. I went to the other side and wiped her sweat off like he had. She jerked her head away, stepping back, and Branhan spoke to her. He told me, "Be real slow, she's getting used to all this. Keep one hand on her so she knows where you are."

"Does she have a name?"

"Not yet."

"You should call her Blackie."

"Even though she's a paint?"

"Yeah."

Branhan slid the halter off her face. He touched her ears, whispering to her. "Sounds good to me," he said.

We walked back inside and I turned to go up the stairs. I looked back once at Branhan. His hat was off, his hair damp with sweat. He smiled that quiet smile, not for me but for himself, and walked to the shadows where the couch was.

I lay in bed listening to Blackie graze. It was a calm sound, like beach waves but softer. Hearing, I realized how lonely the yard was without it.

They say the first part of childhood you lose has to do with time. Looking out at the moon, I didn't feel time at all. But I began to guess, with the foolishness of a child, that some lost things have a way of reappearing when you're ready for the

Hired Help

R andall Sneidel ran his church strictly: he threw out the hymnals and the American flag. He put the biggest Bible he could find, ten pounds of it opened to Leviticus, on the altar. No air conditioning because it was a luxury and also it saved on the electric bill.

Randy—he went by Randy—holy as he tried to be, did hold one thorn in his side: Griffin's BBQ. The cinderblock dive stood only a mile from the church, and this day Randy sat at his usual table, tie slid between two of his shirt buttons, napkin tucked into his collar, looking out over an ancient, rusting horse-drawn combine in the yard opposite. He ate his usual plate: pulled pork on a bun and slathered with pepper-flaked, dark mustard sauce, a cup of Brunswick stew spiced with hot sauce from a plain ketchup squirter marked "M. hot," baked beans and fatback, sweet coleslaw, and two gleaming buttered cornmeal hoecakes to sop it all afterward. Though a barbeque meal couldn't redeem much of anything, that food persuaded Randy that mankind wasn't completely flawed after all.

The preacher sat back sated, sipping from an enormous Coke cup of sweet tea, when Elroy "Bubba" T. Raines pushed the door open. Elroy "Bubba" T. Raines had been employed as a construction subcontractor until, a few weeks before, he had spoken to his boss and client about the low quality of conduit laid in one of his jobs at an elementary school. Perhaps because expertise is unusual in his position, or because his boss was a crook, this interaction left Elroy "Bubba" T. Raines on his own, work-wise. Something about him must have looked competent, because Randy saw in his person the solution to a handful of his church problems.

"Say friend, you wouldn't be looking for a job, now, would you?" said Randy, with his biggest grin.

Elroy "Bubba" T. Raines studied the preacher. Randy looked to him like a cartoon bird. "Yessir, I could use that job," said Elroy "Bubba" T. Raines.

The spinning fan blew Randy's hair off his bald spot. He said "Wonderful."

Randy was a literal man who understood the power of words and the rarity of truth. What's more, he understood that much of the world ran on lies which, the liars not being content with obfuscating the present, bled out to history and future. The more he studied this untruthfulness, the more of it Randy noticed. It drove him a little crazy, but wouldn't an honest search for truth drive anyone crazy? So, Randy cut: he put the thin corner of his old straight razor to certain passages in certain books, slicing out lies one by one. To him this was a rational, if extreme, response. In his calmer moments, Randy thought of it as a war of attrition against falsehood. Once, for example, he found a book called *Cruising through History* in the Delia library and cut Jesus right out of it. Randy walked out of doctor's offices, when he went to the doctor, with whole magazines that he later burned. It was futile to think he could erase all the lies, but Randy tried valiantly. He considered himself a crusader for the truth.

Elroy "Bubba" T. Raines did not quite fit into the passenger side seat of Randy's car. Even if it weren't full altar dressings headed for the pawn shop, the back wouldn't have been big enough for him either. Eventually he packed in and they drove through a pecan orchard to a dirt road to Randy's church: The Tabernacle of the Word: A King James Version Bible-Believing Church: Pastor Randall Sneidel.

The building was low, crooked on sills that bore antique sawmill cuts, its boards soaked through with some unhealthy varnish from the last century. The front steps, objects of the day's pursuit, sagged under years of heavy trespass.

Randy told Elroy "Bubba" T. Raines, "I need you to cut some new boards and replace these old gray, warped ones."

Elroy "Bubba" T. Raines did not mind Randy's desperation—he was used to it from clients. So, there was only one answer he needed. "How much are you going to pay?"

"The laborer deserves his dues," Randy said, and gazed at Elroy "Bubba" T. Raines in a way that did not welcome further questions.

"You got lumber and tools?"

"Lumber's over there," Randy said, pointing to a scrap pile he'd dragged from under the church. Some of the boards bore the marks of single bevel axes. Randy added, "Tools are laid out on the landing." There was an old handsaw, hammer, and nails Randy had pulled from the scrap boards or found in a few jars in the closet. Elroy "Bubba" T. Raines made a low whistle, thinking this was some mess he wound up in. But perhaps a mess that would keep him going for the next week.

"You ain't got no power tools?"

"We don't even have electricity." The church didn't seem to have electricity, but that was because the lines came through dense pines at the rear of the building. Randy hardly ever used the lights.

"Now sir," said Elroy "Bubba" T. Raines, "I don't mean to press a point, but seeing how your tools are less than desirable and your lumber ain't much better, how much are you going to pay me for this?"

"Ten dollars."

Elroy "Bubba" T. Raines muttered what might have been a curse, returning to the dirt road.

"Fifteen."

This time it was a curse.

"All right, twenty-five."

Elroy "Bubba" T. Raines stood with a very skeptical set to his jaw. "I can do it for thirty."

Randy, who knew exactly what thirty dollars could buy at the grocery store, became upset. "I can run right back to Griffin's or Big John's and find six men better at this than you and pay any one of them—"

Elroy "Bubba" T. Raines turned around like he was tired of this shit, because he was. For years he had wanted to leave construction and, incidentally, pursue ministry. Often Elroy "Bubba" T. Raines made up sermons in his mind while he worked. Perhaps, he thought, today was a sign to begin something different.

"All right! Thirty."

"In cash."

"In cash."

Elroy "Bubba" T. Raines set to work, measuring with a piece of string the length and width of the old steps, sawing the old boards, and balancing them on the landing's rail. He produced a wood-tipped cigar that then hung from his lip as he laid down the pieces for fit. Randy watched him from the vestibule, having gone inside not to stand around while Elroy "Bubba" T. Raines worked.

Randy studied this man, whom he had underestimated. There is always some jealousy in men who cannot manually fix things for those who can. Randy wondered if the man was dishonest. The preacher definitely did not appreciate his help singing, as Elroy "Bubba" T. Raines began to do, about a crawling king snake.

In half an hour the job was finished. The dull gray of the old boards clashed with the rest of the wood but they fit well so Randy was pleased. Elroy "Bubba" T. Raines said, "Here's your steps. Pay me."

Randy gazed at the sky as though taking in the day. "It still isn't too hot yet. Don't you think you could do another job? I've got some shingles missing on the roof."

Elroy "Bubba" T. Raines twisted the wood tip of the cigar in his mouth. "Fifty."

The image of a fifty-dollar bill in his mind made sweat appear on Randy's brow. "Now we are just a poor humble church, we can't really afford these repairs, but it leaks on us rainy Sunday mornings—"

"Fifty."

"If you could find it in your heart—"

"Fifty, cash."

"Out of your generosity—"

"I got the right to name the price of my labor just like you got the right to find some other dummy if you don't like it."

Randy's jaw ached from clenching as he watched Elroy "Bubba" T. Raines climb the ladder.

Elroy "Bubba" T. Raines' work boots thudded on the roof above. His hammer blows shook the joists, sending down little streams of dust. Randy hadn't told him of the wasp nest hanging under the back eave and decided to keep the secret.

A truck rumbled into the lot. Randy peered from the window. A dog panted in the cab. The driver stuck his head out the window and said, "Hey Bubba, what are you doing way out here?"

"One thing after another. How about you? This ain't the way to Big John's."

"I was going to pay Diane a visit."

"Uh-huh."

Randy cringed and moved to the side of the window. He recognized Dale, his former roommate.

Dale read over the sign from his truck, studied the gray steps and near-black doors. "This is a piece of work."

Elroy "Bubba" T. Raines climbed down to speak to the man. "It looks like hell," he said. "Don't know why he don't just build a new one. He could get one of those steel buildings like that Church of Christ in Vienna. I went to a revival in that one. It looked real nice." When Elroy "Bubba" T. Raines imagined having his own church, he wasn't sure if he preferred a new, spacious, carpeted building like the one he described or one of the historic, wood-paneled AME churches downtown.

Randy stormed out of the vestibule, past his table full of tracts and out the front door.

Elroy "Bubba" T. Raines leaned with one elbow on the truck's door, looking at Randy like no matter what the preacher did, he wouldn't be impressed.

"I'm not paying you to entertain company," Randy said.

"You want me to leave, then?"

Randy looked from Dale, who held back wicked laughter, to Elroy "Bubba" T. Raines, to the roof. A few shingles lay skewed where he hadn't placed them yet. Randy had concerned himself with written lies for so long that he forgot how flesh and blood could lie. His help wouldn't do the job as it should be done, efficiently and with respect, but had to make Randy look like a fool. What was he to do when faced with such facetious dishonesty? Randy took off his jacket and climbed the ladder. He could feel the other men's eyes from below, the tension between them waiting to laugh.

The roof had more of a pitch than Randy had thought. He went on all fours up what seemed a great distance to the place where his help had been mending. Some shingles on either side weren't nailed all the way, through laziness or some inscrutable system that the man used. Randy grabbed the closest new shingle. It was so heavy that he almost lost his balance laying it in place. There was a snort from below.

Three wasps hung in the air beside Randy. He kept a sidelong gaze on them, watching them watch him like little tempting devils.

The shingle fit in one line of them and Randy aligned the lower edge and put five nails in it before he saw that the others only had three. He lined another shingle up to discover that the first had a downhill cast of a few inches. When he ripped it back up, the nails tore right through the middle of the tar paper, creating a gash that wouldn't hold a shower. Randy tried to nail it in anyhow and hit his thumb. He did not show it—Randy was very good at hiding his own pain. In a lying world there was no one he could trust with it.

So Randy hammered, shingle after crooked shingle, until he felt the sun beat on his bald head and the knees of his pants burned from the gravely shingles. His BBQ lunch turned and growled in his stomach and he felt pitiful.

Finished, he climbed down the ladder. The two men had not moved, as though they had nothing else to do all day but watch him. Elroy "Bubba" T. Raines leaned to one side to see the job Randy had done. The dog leaned with him. "You're going to need to tar some of those nail holes over," he said. "I can do it for ten more dollars." Elroy "Bubba" T. Raines thought this was perhaps cruel but said it anyway. By then he had decided ministry was not for him.

The man in the truck shook.

Randy pulled cash from his wallet and placed it in Elroy "Bubba" T. Raines' hand. His help counted it, licking his thumb to turn each bill, and nodded. The look he gave Randy was the kindest it'd been all day. Trust didn't begin on a job until money changed hands.

Elroy "Bubba" T. Raines took a tar gun from the back of the truck, which was full of tools. He finished the job in minutes. Up the ladder with no hands, a few practiced lines over the gashes. Elroy "Bubba" T. Raines did it well but he didn't make a show of it, thinking Randy was upset enough already. There was just something about the preacher that Elroy "Bubba" T. Raines couldn't help but mess with him. Randy's kind of seriousness had to be balanced out. Plus the preacher looked miserable.

Soon Elroy "Bubba" T. Raines was in the truck with Dale churning dust back toward Griffin's. Randy watched them go and turned to his church. The new patches gleamed on the roof like insect carapaces. The steps glowed in the noon heat, a burning path to the door.

Randy sensed something fundamentally wrong with the world. Perhaps the lies had gone further than he knew. Taking up the massive altar Bible, he passed its pages along until he came to a certain part. There, at the Cana wedding where Jesus turned water into wine, he set the point of his razor to the page and cut because drinking was a sin and so Jesus could have nothing to do with it. He had never cut the Bible itself but here was a lie, even in the Word. Randy cut more: the suppers with whores and drunks, the con-man Zacchaeus in the tree, and Mary Magdalene who shouldn't even be touching Jesus with her impure hands. Randy piled these scraps along with others he cut into an ancient offering plate and set them on fire. Bit by bit passages passed into the flame, crumbling their heavy English into something that looked like Greek and finally to gray dust.

When the last page had succumbed to the flame and vanished, Randy held the finished work, his act of bringing order to a broken world. He carried it reverently to the altar and placed it there, open to the death of Jesus, and moved among the pews with his razor, gutting Bible after Bible, until the leaves lay on the ground as under a dead tree. He sat in a middle pew, feeling a little better—cleansed perhaps—and prayed to God, which made him feel a little less lonely.

That One Time Barry Got Ahold of the Gun

I knew it was bad but I was too drunk to tell how bad when Barry raked back the receiver of the AK-type rifle I kept in the closet. He laughed, the bastard. Sure, I kept it close by with a full mag, but not one in the chamber. I'm not one of those rednecks.

There was a fire outside. Donny and Jason, the calmest of us, stood before it drinking the good whiskey Donny had brought. Across the fire from them, Jake passed his arms through the yellow flame. He claimed he would walk on the coals. "I will master the fire," he said. About four of us stood around him, and asked why. "As the great George Mallory said, 'Because it's there.'" Then Jake added, " . . . bitches." Laughter roared like the fire we built and built, the sparks from each new log spinning into a summer sky, so bright it hid the stars. We pulled old wood pallets onto the fire. We pulled the junk from my lumber shed into the fire. We pulled the yard scrap pile into the fire. Jason had brought his pistol that shot four-ten shotshells and he discharged it into the yard scraps in case a snake was there. He was probably the soberest among us.

We found the body of a snake and hoisted it. I swung it above our heads, slinging droplets of serpent blood onto faces and shirts. The shirts came off. The fire was large—the fire was huge. I pitched the snake's body into the fire. We gloated as it curled on itself. The smell made us crazy. Someone started the dance as a joke, and then we shuffled, we kicked, we raised hands around the fire. Circled, shouted. Yelled the names of our fathers, our mothers, our wives, our children. Sang them. Jake cursed the snake, his chest tight in the flame light as though he drew every bit of venom from his marrow to spit it back. Jake kicked the fire. He beat the ends of logs with his hands. While we danced, having forgotten who we were, Jake leaped across the fire. Jake danced across the fire. He was in it, around it, its priest.

And then Barry came out spraying tracers into the sky, trying to shoot God.

If He Ever Could Get Free

There were times Branhan looked out over their six acres of pine-dotted ranch field, bordered by neighbors who got drunk and loud sometimes and kept dogs chained to trees in the yard, not with hate but unbearable loneliness. He'd thought about it. There was the vast West: sun-bleached, mystical New Mexico, or the tawny solitude of Wyoming, or Colorado where the mountains stood like ancient, mighty angels. He thought Texas, but then remembered how they'd been about gay people. Austin maybe, but Branhan had it in his heart to be a real rancher, not some culture cowboy.

He wanted the running and the sweat-smell of horses. To know them and have the hard-won time to do it. Or Branhan dreamed to forsake the horses themselves. Maybe he'd buy a motorcycle. Maybe he'd brew beer or hike the Appalachian trail or take a string of lovers. No more feeding twice a day, staying up nights with a colicked mare, no more self-subjugation to the needs of twenty animals.

But who would he be without them?

He could leave, though, any day he wanted to.

Demme wasn't Branhan's first lover, but he was the one who lasted. While pitching hay, while driving home in the early morning, Branhan thought on how their being together was twice a transgression. "Love goes deeper than any of us can guess, and the only choice in falling in love is to fall along with it or pass it up." He wrote that in a leather journal his mother had given him.

Branhan found his father, Frank, laid out in an empty stall, his breathing shallow and welts covering his arms and face. Branhan gasped a yell. His father was dense, heavy, and strong from a life lived working, but Branhan dragged him up into a fireman carry and into the house and onto the bed. In the light he looked worse. Branhan's breath couldn't fill him. He dialed 9-1-1 on his cell phone. They asked if his father was allergic to bees, to wasps, to hornets. He knew his father was fine with bees—they never stung him, even when he came close to the wild hives in the woods—but he didn't know about the others.

Branhan asked him, "What was it like back then?"

"Back then," Arnie repeated. His eyes lit from the window like hot forge irons.

"In the old days. For us."

"Us?"

Branhan rode in the ambulance. His father's eyes were closed but he breathed. The emergency room was a place of linoleum-echoed wailing, electronic beeps and whirrs. They brought Frank in with a rattle of gurney wheels. They took him away and told Branhan to wait. He sat and pulled his book, one about old-time loggers in Montana, out of his jacket pocket. The words on the page didn't do a thing. Branhan only sat holding it and worrying.

His father had been stung twenty-seven times by hornets. He wasn't allergic but after that many stings it didn't matter. Once they treated him and got him into a room, which he shared with three others, the nurses allowed Branhan to see him. Frank sat awake with a thin sheen of sweat on his forehead. The blisters of the stings pocked him like a plague.

"How you feeling?" Branhan asked.

"Like I lost that fight. We ought to keep a tennis racket in the barn."

"Did they get you in the barn?"

"Yeah. I was digging through that pile of old lead ropes and turns out they'd been building a nest in there. I had Merlin tied in the bay and they got him too. He spooked and jumped and hollered so I couldn't get by until I could finally grab hold of the knot and pull him loose. That's the last thing I remember."

Rain spat from a black sky, drumming on the horse trailer and twinkling in the arena lights. Thunder cracked close by.

In the middle of someone's pattern in Branhan's class, a transformer had popped two hundred yards away. The lights failed. The horse bucked its rider and cantered willy-nilly across the arena. Blackie, Branhan's horse, startled and bucked. Branhan pulled her head around and spoke to her. Frank stood from the bench, about to leap forward to grab the horse.

They could still hear drunk riders yelling from the stalls.

"Anybody with sense ought to know it's wrong."

"You can't rely on people having sense. The horses should be able to handle a thunderstorm anyway."

Some of the men had looked at Branhan in that way he'd begun to recognize. He didn't understand how they knew. He sure hadn't seen any of them at Charlie's but maybe he had. And half of them were drunk.

Rain misted the town as he drove. The skipped training sessions hovered in his mind; all those responsibilities.

Branhan drove his father home once the nurses released him. He had to rest a few days. Branhan fed all the horses, mucked the stalls, turned out and brought in those who needed it. Merlin showed some welts through his winter coat but only three or four. He sure didn't act like he was hurting. Blackie caught his eye and he felt ashamed for not working her. He'd planned to show her the lariat so that some days later he could begin teaching her roping. The round pen lights would give him time. Branhan didn't stay to train the horse.

Instead he drove through the close, dark woods. No shops this time, no pool halls or bars. Nothing until Charlie's, because nothing else was anything like home. He repeated like a mantra his idea: he could leave anytime, anytime he wanted.

Frank hadn't been to church since Branhan's mother passed, but he still remembered his share of Psalms and Bible verses from growing up Baptist. Every now and then he muttered these under his breath while he shoveled horse shit, or he'd recite them to the horses while he brushed them. The only ones he quoted to Branhan were the passage from Job , "Hast thou given the horse strength, and clothed his neck with thunder?" and once when they drove through foggy Tennessee, "Lord, touch the mountains and they shall smoke." They didn't talk much about God except that He made the earth and the horses.

"I want to understand."

"What did you say?"

"I want to understand, sir." Branhan finally met Arnie's gaze, mustering his strength.

Arnie watched him.

Branhan went out to work with Blackie one day under crisp white cloud and a sky blue as it must've been the very day God made it. Branhan wanted to make a cutting horse out of her because she had cow-sense and knew to track. It might take a while.

The steam from her nostrils was white and new as the cloud above. Mounted, there was only the compass turning, that feeling that they had the same balance. The posts of her legs crushed into the soil. *You have more to you than these tame ones—you are like the wide prairie you came from.* Circles to the right, narrow to wide, circles back the way they'd come.

Branhan sank to the ground. His body felt heavier, reduced to human legs. Blackie was calm in all but the bedrock-gray depths of her eyes, that part he would never know. *Thank you. In whatever secret name you bear, I thank you.*

She taught him what horse training meant, what the depth of it was. To speak to something wild, a part of creation that could and might kill him, and to have it listen and speak back, was the most profound experience of Branhan's life. More profound than love. Perhaps as profound as loving through two transgressions.

There was the day when he was fifteen, Branhan filled his wallet with his cash savings, put it in the inside pocket of his coat, and began walking the seven miles to town, intent on catching a greyhound bus there or else a ride to the Amtrak station in Macon. No incident or abuse prompted this trip. No unkindness from his father, nor even bad behavior from the horses. His mother had been gone by then for two years. At some nopoint in the road, above a ditch filled and jagged with cut-back pine limbs, Branhan stopped. He shifted his weight. Finally, he turned and walked the five miles back.

Branhan felt loose as he drove past the reaches of town through fields of harvested cotton or fallow ones with bits of peanut leaves dried along the rows. It felt good, maybe, to have a taste of what it'd be like if he ever could get free of the farm. No more weekends devoted to horse shows or worrying about getting back to feed. He could leave it anytime he wanted.

"He didn't look that bad when I fed him."

"That's because they got me first." Frank gazed past the end of the bed. "You know, the doctor told me forty people a year die from hornet stings in Japan. But they got bigger hornets than we do."

They sat. Branhan couldn't seem to swallow. His father seemed okay apart from the big welts on his skin. A few times he made to scratch one of the sores and stopped himself.

"Where were you today, son?"

"I got in late—"

"What kept you?"

"I was talking to somebody."

He nodded. Frank didn't know many of his friends because a lot of them were from Charlie's. He said, "The animals come first, son."

"I know, sir."

Branhan flushed. This wasn't at all what he'd imagined. He said quietly, "For gay people."

Arnie glared. He had a way of looking at someone as though everything they said was the most stupid thing ever said. "You mean all us fags? One big, happy, family?" Arnie drew out a Pall Mall and lit it with a lighter from the pack.

"I suppose so. Sir."

"Why the hell do you want to know that? Hell, you can probably get married today if you wanted to. If you drive far enough. Start you up a nice life with a three-bedroom house and crepe myrtles in the front yard."

"Then why didn't you do it?" Frank's tone was harsh, disappointed. Maybe hurt. "You got to be there to feed, son. They can't take care of themselves."

"I know, Dad—"

"Sir."

"I know that, sir."

They were quiet. Someone else in the room, behind a curtain, coughed. Frank said, "You never done that before. What was so important it made you start today?"

"I told you, I was with a friend."

"A girl?"

"No, nothing like that. I was talking to a friend."

"About what?"

"The past," Branhan said. Then he looked at his father. The man's face was tanned except for a line across his forehead where he wore his hat. Creases branched from his eyes. The skin on his cheeks was only then beginning to slack but it didn't diminish him. His father was the strongest man he'd ever known. What must it be like, Branhan wondered, to walk with confidence in the world?

Or what would it be like if he got cut off from him, and had to face the world alone?

His father looked back at him. He said, "The past comes after the animals are taken care of."

"Yes, sir," Branhan said, and they talked about the chores he'd pick up if there was to be a hospital stay.

One night, but it could have been any night, Branhan looked over Demme's clothes. "You ain't been having to hoof it, have you?"

"No, no, I'm under a roof."

"You would tell me."

Demme smiled to himself.

They danced close, in the press of close dancers. Branhan feeling Demme's neck against his cheek, breathing into the warmth there, the reality of him who so often seemed like a dream. He dreamed of what it'd be like to wake up next to Demme at five when he usually went to feed the horses. Of knowing he'd be there night after night. They hadn't talked about family.

"They should have called it off."

"You're right."

"Then why'd we stay?"

Branhan and his father tromped through the barn putting horses safely in their stalls. In the house, his father poured himself a glass of whiskey distilled in nearby Americus and poured Branhan one too.

"I told you," Frank said. Wind tussled the azalea bushes. "We gave our word. Because tonight was a special test, above and beyond the show."

"What about the horses? Keeping them safe?"

His father hummed a noise. "I know." He continued, "It was a test for them too, and they were brave. There are things that come along that aren't safe, and some of them are worth doing. Some are about the only things worth doing." The old man took a sip. "Imagine the old war horses. Would a Kiowa war horse or his rider worry about riding in that tonight?"

"There haven't been war horses for eighty years, Dad. Not since machine guns."

"There must be some. Maybe in the older places of the world."

Branhan said, "I remember Bush's Defense of Marriage Act and I remember folks boycotting movies because they had gay people in them. I remember seeing those damn 'God Hates Fags' people everywhere on the news. I remember the line out the door of Chick-fil-a stretched a block. But it seems like things are changing. Maybe not here, but some places." Now Branhan leaned in, not by much, but straight-backed as his father had drilled him to be. He said, "But you lived through the harder times. I want to know."

Arnie took a wet gulp of his beer. "You want to know about that, you need to buy me a motherfucking real drink."

When he drove to Charlie's the first time, Branhan parked across the street and half a block away. He sat in his car, watching the neon sign like an old honky-tonk, the way people crossed the parking lot like they couldn't be in the outside air long. Or they couldn't breathe until they got inside. After a long time, Branhan rubbed a scuff out of his boot toe on his jeans, put on his hat, and crossed the street.

Up front there was a coat check and the man attending it looked Branhan up and down. Branhan nodded to him and entered the rest of the bar, half of it dance floor packed with line-dancers, the other half pool tables and booths, ringed by a bar of shellacked pine boards, all of it under Alan Jackson and slide guitar and neon beer signs. The people dancing wore clothes like the cowboy stuff Branhan wore but nicer and newer and better-fitting. When he went to the bar for a beer, the bartender walked away from flirting with, or being flirted with by, someone in a dress and boa with a close-trimmed beard and earrings.

Branhan didn't mind working a room, but he didn't know what to call some of these people, what pronouns to use. It wasn't just etiquette—he genuinely didn't know what gender some of them were. If any. So he leaned back by the pool tables observing and sipping beer, until a person—AJ—who seemed female-bodied except for a full beard, asked for a game of pool.

Branhan played, talking with AJ about where they were each from, about his horses. AJ sunk the 8-ball, they clinked glasses, and AJ went away to a different group. Branhan never heard AJ use a pronoun to clarify themselves so he didn't either.

Later, after more beer, Branhan danced. He went back the next week, and the next, and the next, until he learned the names of the bartenders, until the coat-check guy finally nodded to see him. Branhan danced with a man there for the first time. There were many firsts.

Town faded and Branhan came to the black and poor part of town, past houses with dirt yards and projects. Brightly painted storefronts advertised pool halls and dance clubs, tire places. Branhan wondered if Demme had been to those kinds of clubs, or what it was like for him if he did. Demme was more open than Branhan, more obvious. He had a hard time picturing his lover in some of these places where the world got strict about what men were supposed to do and be.

Shuddering through the gears on that loose transmission, Branhan thought through every possibility he'd come up with for his life: a ranch in Montana or Texas, or moving to Atlanta, or out to St. Simons or someplace on the coast where he'd be safer than in Savannah, but maybe Savannah too. And what he might do: hire on at an honest-to-God ranch where they still drove cattle from horseback, or go to vet or farrier school, or say the hell with it and be an electrician, a carpenter, a pipefitter. One of his friends was a welder who had gone to Iraq, where the government paid him $90,000 a year to weld steel drums in the desert. Or the military, for that matter.

Blackie was a mustang and she was being that and a half in the round pen. She huffed, she charged, and didn't seem to care when Branhan threw his lariat at her chest to stop her. He went and got a lunge whip. That only pissed her off more. Finally, Branhan cooled her with a walk and led her back to her stall. It took five whole minutes to get her to go through the gate without crowding him. Branhan's knuckles were white on the lead rope and he cussed her in a gentle, reassuring voice that, he felt sure, meant nothing to her.

He didn't have any lessons that day and had plans to work the string of horses he and his father owned but after Blackie and that damned horse show the night before and the cold rain that came out of nowhere halfway through feeding, Branhan climbed into his truck. He beat his bootheels against the steel runner to knock the mud off and pulled out of the drive.

He could do it. He could leave anytime.

Would they be able to walk down the street together in Atlanta? Savannah? Somewhere like Wyoming or Texas, would Branhan need to carry and keep a shotgun by the door?

Blackie was a mustang, hardly domesticated, but mostly tamed.

Branhan had felt it, even if he didn't know what it was: the way some of the men at horse shows looked at him, the way he'd wanted to spend every free moment of fourth grade with Will

Carson. Maybe the way he had begun to feel the horses more deeply than the other trainers—but then, his father had that too.

Finally—it felt like finally—he told his Aunt Rose some of this while they drank cheap pinot noir on her porch. She listened. Branhan spoke like trying to put two north ends of a magnet together, avoiding by habit and felt necessity the utterance that would change him, and his life, and his family. He breathed to calm his shaking hands. If Aunt Rose had looked at him too knowingly, too accommodatingly, Branhan felt he might have shattered. He didn't want to, but he would've. Instead Aunt Rose's look was easy, it was kind. Like a friend's over wine, which they were. They sat while a train rattled along the tracks across the street. Aunt Rose began telling Branhan about Charlie's, as easily as a friend would recommend a well-loved novel.

Branhan went to the hardware store for odds and ends they'd needed for a while and he thought about working there. He went to the farming co-op for a new pair of jeans and thought the same thing. His father had encouraged him to work at a place like that when he was in high school, to dip his feet in the working world. Instead Branhan taught riding lessons.

One of the bars looked open. It was 11:00 am. Branhan pulled into the lot. He left his hat in the car and ran his fingers through his hair.

There were four people in the bar, five counting the bartender. An old man in a driving cap and sunglasses sat by a jukebox. Two younger guys in baggy jeans sprawled in a booth. They wore flat-bill caps at angles and sat before open tallboys. The first looked up at him in utter confusion and his friend turned around with the same reaction. A guy in a blazer at the bar didn't seem to care one way or the other. The bartender looked up once and went back to wiping down the counter. He said, "What you want, Garth Brooks?"

The young guys snickered. The old men kept smoking.

Branhan walked to the bar. His boots sounded like horses walking. "High Life tallboy, like them."

The bartender bent and dug into a cooler for the beer can. He opened it and placed it before Branhan. He took and drank a solid guzzle. One of the young guys said in a kind of stage whisper, "Damn, Garth Brooks wanting to get drunk."

The other, in country twang singsong: "It's five o'clock somewhere." They snickered more. The well-dressed man cracked a smile.

The bartender peered at Branhan. He wore a thin mustache that fit his narrow face. "Go easy, Texas Ranger. I got a policy about getting drunk here."

The jokers: "Texas Ranger. Bruce Lee go'n come in here and kick his ass."

"Anybody want to buy a Bowflex?"

Branhan said, "I ain't getting drunk." He studied the worn hardwood bar.

"Um, sir, I believe you have tracked cattle manure into this establishment."

"Dude been walking on cow pies."

The bartender hung by Branhan, perhaps thinking he'd leave quickly. Branhan, not disagreeing, took large gulps of his beer. "How long you been here?"

"You mean me, or this bar?" The bartender spoke softly, just between the two of them.

"Either."

"I was born in Valdosta, lived here thirty years. Bar's been here since 1947."

"That long?"

"That long."

"You don't get many white folks here, I suppose."

"Nope. Every now and then. Funny how it don't look too different from the days of Jim Crow when it started."

Branhan peered at the bartender and gave a solemn nod. He took a last guzzle of his beer and left a five on the bar to cover drink and tip. As he passed the jokers, he said "It'd be horse shit, more likely." They had nearly forgotten about him, turned instead to their cell phones. On his way out Branhan heard one sing, "Like a horse-shit cowboy. . ." and the other break into a fresh laugh.

"Let me drive," Demme said.

"You ain't been out there."

"You can tell me the way, can't you?"

"I don't know what Dad would do if somebody like you—"

"I'm the same as you. Or did you forget?"

Branhan paused. Thinking hurt. He said, "I mean, he ain't never said nothing, or not much, but you know, he grew up here."

Demme gave Branhan that look that went through him. "I'll take my chances."

Soon Branhan slumped into the passenger seat of his truck while Demme pulled onto the highway. Branhan said, "It's that you're black as much as it is gay."

"Oh it is? Is your daddy racist?"

He took the highway to Albany without thinking. The interstate might have been a temptation, or an escape route saved for when he did decide to leave.

Along the way Branhan turned on the radio, spinning the dial through country and Christian stations which were hard to tell apart. Willie Nelson sang and Branhan remembered another lyric: *the dream of every man is to know how freedom feels.* Maybe the old man could bless him to leave, but how would Branhan ask? His family tree contained little now but the one stout branch of his father. Without him, Branhan would be rootless, drifting downriver as a wanderer. Maybe being that kind of person, a man with no name, would be better.

At first the freedom was exhilarating. But Branhan, from time to time, felt a gut-twisting shame. He couldn't abide shame. Did that shame come from his own heart or from the world? His father had told him, two things you don't take from anybody you don't trust: shame and praise.

Branhan only wanted to be there, to be with these who were, he supposed, his people.

Branhan came through the young pine lots, the abandoned gas stations, to Albany, and then to Charlie's. It was one o'clock.

The bar was open but dreary. Natural light didn't suit the place. Only a handful of older folks hung out there, not unlike the old men at the black folks' bar. Branhan recognized Arnie, a spindly man who tended to be drunk by the time everyone else got to the bar and too drunk once the dancing started. Branhan and Demme and their friends had laughed at him. Now he looked like a familiar face. Branhan got two beers and sat at the booth with Arnie, passing one over.

Arnie was thin, his long limbs dark from working outside. The darkness of his face highlighted his gray-green eyes. When he looked into those eyes now, Branhan feared he had made a serious mistake. There was something he had never noticed, something dangerous about Arnie. The man said with coldness, "To what do I owe this courtesy?" Branhan broke his gaze. He couldn't have held it.

"Well, young man?" asked Arnie, leaning and drinking without taking his eyes off Branhan.

"What do you want?"

"Dry Beefeater up with a twist. And you tell him all that." Then, "Fuck it, get two of them."

Branhan went to the bartender, a sleepy bearish guy, and told him. The man cut his eyes to Arnie but made the drink and poured it in a plastic cup. While he did, Branhan bought a pack of Marlboro Reds from the machine and lit one the moment he got the pack open.

Arnie had finished his beer and he took a deep sip from the martini. He didn't look at Branhan but out the textured-glass window.

"You know about Stonewall?" Arnie asked.

"I do."

Sun from the window lit Arnie's face, casting shadows off his sharp features. He said, "Queens in drag made a kick line against New York cops in riot helmets. Like some queer-ass Pickett's charge."

Branhan listened. Arnie continued, "You couldn't be out back then, that's for sure. Not around here. Nobody called themselves queer. It was something you got called. Before they beat you, sometimes. The *hoi polloi* and the sheriff both.

"The churches didn't talk about it until the sixties and they didn't get really ugly about it until the eighties with all that Reagan and Graham bullshit. The problem was, they all thought us gay folks were coming from San Fran or Houston to corrupt the young people. See, they thought we all showed up during Civil Rights, and that made 'queer' just another word for 'nigger-lover.'" Arnie turned to him with that look that had been, Branhan realized, intentionally filed and sharpened over time. "I mean 'n-word lover,' excuse me." Arnie paused, measuring Branhan's response. He'd seen Branhan and Demme together, Branhan realized. Of course he had.

"The people didn't realize, or they couldn't believe, that we'd been there all along. Hell, my first time was in a movie theater in Tifton." Arnie chuckled, then laughed as though something had caught him. It went on for a minute, dry laughter like branches cracking, and a tear rolled from Arnie's eye. He collected himself, as much as it seemed like he ever did, and drank down the rest of the first martini and a sip of the second. "That was a long time back. But people knew. It's taking them a while to get used to us being out in the open about it. But they've known for a long time."

Was that blackness a real part of the man Branhan loved, or only more of the world getting between them as it did? Branhan might never know it. He might not even be welcome to know.

Branhan's mouth was dry. He asked, "How'd your folks take it?"

"Oh Lord."

"If you don't want to—"

"No. Hell, I'm spilling my damn guts anyway." Arnie lit a new cigarette and took a solid gulp of his drink. He said, "I told my momma first. She about had an aneurysm and the next time I talked to her she asked me if I had the AIDS. That what she called it, 'The AIDS.' I don't think she believed me when I told her I didn't even though I checked it eight times that year. She started telling me all the terrible mess the radio told her, how it meant I was an atheist and wanted to have sex with kids and all that—I think those damn radio preachers are the fucked-up ones. All I do is like men instead of women and they're the ones coming up with this shit that'll make your skin crawl. You know some of those crazy-asses in Uganda or wherever, those places they'll fucking put a gay man in front of a firing squad, it's because the preachers there tell everybody that gay people eat shit and fuck infants. And American missionaries go over there and tell them, great job, great job! I hope they goddamn eat shit. I don't believe in hell or none of that but when I think of those people I hope there's a damn hell, fire and brimstone and all."

Arnie took a long draw. He finished his martini. "Get me another beer, young man."

Branhan did so.

"I had to have this conversation with my momma that no, I didn't want to have sex with children, and me and the Lord were fine, and I even went to that MCC church in Augusta when I was up that way. After probably a month of proving I hadn't turned into some kind of ass-chasing Frankenstein, I got to tell her my side of the story. I sent her some of my books. Next thing I knew, momma wanted to come with me to Pride in Atlanta. She was converted."

"What about your dad?"

"He passed away."

"I'm sorry."

"It's all right." He sat for a while, quiet. "We never patched up. If that's even what you'd call it."

Arnie said that easily enough. His shoulders rose with a deep breath, one Branhan recognized as the type you can never breath out all the way.

Branhan came through the dark lot into the glowing heart of Charlie's and drank four shots in his first ten minutes. A young guy in a new straw hat laughed at the first two and quit laughing at the third. Branhan joined a line dance. He played pool and missed half his licks on the cue ball. At some point he switched to beer and lost track of how many he drank. It wasn't more than five. It wasn't much less.

Demme rushed and found him in a booth toward the back.

"Branhan—"

"I texted you." The words rolled out of Branhan's mouth.

"I know, you've been texting like hell. How many have you had?"

"I had shots of whiskey." The room became a wash of woodgrain, blue neon, and people moving in blurry shapes past them.

"How you feel?"

"I got the spins."

Demme held him. Branhan's head lolled onto his shoulder. Demme said, "What the hell made you do this?"

Branhan said, "Bees," and then lost all memory.

There was the time a few years before his mother passed when they built a fire in a low place of the pasture and sat out on aged quilts and wool blankets, one of them his grandfather's from the war, Branhan and his father and his mother, to watch a meteor shower. Lizzie set potatoes and onion in tin foil to bake in the coals while his father set a steel grate over the coals to grill shish-kabobs. They wrapped themselves in one blanket then, late into the night and cold, but the fire warmed them. Even the cold at Branhan's back seemed of a piece with it. They ate with their hands in the dark, breaking off portions of baked and salted potato or, once it cooled, eating from the spud. Carefully they slid steak and peppers and Vidalia onion off hot skewers. After they finished, Frank grinned and snuck a steel flask out of his pocket to glint in the firelight. "Frank," Branhan's mother said. "It's the Lagavulin, Lizzie. Boy's old enough to know what good whisky's like." She looked at Branhan. "You can if you want. You don't have to." "I'll try it." Frank produced two enamel mugs concealed for the purpose and poured with great care. Branhan's mother said, "Hell, pour me one too." Father and son looked at her. Lizzie looked back. "Yes, I mean it." The stars fell overhead, to the silence and the crickets and the horses clipping grass and blowing. The three of them around their fire together, their own small star.

Branhan woke with his whole body reeling. When he finally made sense of the motel room around him, he sat up to an instant, jarring headache.

"What time is it?" Branhan asked.

"About seven forty-five," Demme said. "And good morning to you too."

"Aw hell." Branhan made to get out of bed and didn't make it. His second attempt succeeded but not without a fresh wave of nausea and pain.

Demme said. "You sure you're ready to go?"

Branhan went to the bathroom. He was there a long while. Demme sat drinking his fancy coffee drink. He'd bought Branhan a black coffee but now it seemed like a foregone conclusion. Coming back out, Branhan said, "I got to go home and feed the horses."

"Can't your old man take care of that?"

"The animals come first," Branhan said, looking for his boots. "Anyway he's laid up and he can't."

Demme watched him. After a while he nudged Branhan's other boot toward him with his foot. "You go'n drive all the way back like this?"

"Got to."

Branhan saw where Demme had set his hat on the door handle.

Then Arnie's look again, although Branhan felt it differently, as though it was the hilt of the dagger held toward him now and not the deadly point. "They still hate us. They'll kill us if they can, make no mistake. The South has the heart of a snake. You might can back it into the rocks, but that fucker'll bite yet.

There was the day, and there were many days, when among the horses' snuffling and gentle champing and the darting swallows and the golden sun just pushing through the sky's blue-gray bedclothes and no earthly sound but them that Branhan felt something, felt it bodily and in that inner quiet roominess, that could rightly be called holy.

As soon as Branhan and Demme got to the farm, Branhan went inside. His father was in bed and looked happy from the medication. "You look awful," he told Branhan, who indeed felt awful.

"I didn't sleep real good."

"I'd say not."

"How do you feel?"

"Doped up. Better though. You go'n ride the mustang?"

"Yeah, here in a minute."

Branhan asked him if he wanted anything but since they'd told him he couldn't drink coffee the answer was no. Frank didn't seem to notice Branhan was three hours late.

Branhan's stomach and body and head felt like hell but the work came to him as some sort of healing. The sounds of grain pouring into steel, of hooves on the hollow-sounding earth, the weight of buckets in his arms—they settled into a rhythm, a familiarity. He felt better.

Demme helped feed and petted the horses on their foreheads, which only the Appaloosa liked. The horses put their heads over the fence to look at him. They liked him. Demme sang, making fun of the country station on the barn radio. He seemed to have forgiven Branhan for what he'd said and maybe for drinking like an idiot.

Branhan knew Demme had arrived before he saw him. Looking up, he saw Demme for a moment as a new man, forgetting for a blink that they were together. As Demme came into focus in his mind, that burst of attraction bloomed into the realization that Demme was his, and he was Demme's, so that the two feelings, first of desire running ahead even of sight, then of knowing and grateful belonging, settled in his mind. His neck muscles eased. Perhaps it was because of the transgressions that Branhan knew it was love he felt.

Demme asked, "Is your daddy all right?"

"Yeah. Still groggy on the meds but he's good."

"I'd like to see the house."

"You see it, don't you?"

"I'd like to go in and see it. I'll fix lunch."

"We ain't got much in the fridge."

After some arguing they drove out to the gas station to buy enough food for lunch. Branhan wanted Demme and his father to meet, even though the thought wrapped his guts like a colic. Even though he wanted Demme to see his own room and his grandmother's quilt he used as a bedspread.

They were pouring feed along the fence under a blade of orange cloud that crossed the sunset like it was bigger than the world. Branhan and Frank hadn't said much about Demme's visit, only talked chores, Frank's meds and getting around their effects. Frank had flushed the last half of the painkillers.

Steam blew from the horses' nostrils. Frank gently scolded the ones who pawed. Without looking up at Branhan, he said, "I feel like I've known for a long time. Since you were young."

Branhan froze. "What did I do? Was I—"

"It wasn't anything you did, son. It's who you are. It's your heart." Frank stood and leaned against the wood-rail fence. "And you've got a good heart, son."

Branhan stood near his father, neither of them looking at one another, among the horses eating plainly as though the day was another in the tens of thousands of years of their domestication. His legs didn't tremble but felt airy, like he could, and might, sprint away and keep sprinting.

That night Branhan and Frank drank the Lagavulin and Frank disappeared into the attic for a moment, no idea why, until he returned with a wood tennis racket. "Hornets my ass, that's what this means," he said, and Branhan broke into a laugh like he hadn't in years. It tickled Frank too. They laughed and toasted destruction to hornets and Branhan thought to himself, this is it, if only for this moment. This is how freedom feels.

Around Blackie, Demme became quiet. She didn't have all the mustang out of her yet, which made Branhan wary of her around new people. Demme rubbed caked mud from her cheek and she let him. There is a connection sometimes between a person and a horse, a kind of love at first sight. Branhan watched them. Demme and Blackie, they had it.

Would he ever understand the whole of Demme? Branhan knew the knowing of him. The curve of his hip, how he refused to sip coffee through a plastic lid. What his real laugh sounded like. Them wrapped together in hotel sheets on a night that felt stolen. Them walking together through a swamp forest of ancient cypress and oak; them in the silence and awe of a world where they seemed scarcely to matter. But he felt he barely knew Demme's blackness. By way of family, Branhan had only met one cousin Demme brought to Charlie's whose cousinage was dubious anyway.

The screen door clattered behind them. Demme took in the cherry paneling, the framed horse show pictures, Frank's old '70s recliner.

His father was awake and in decent shape. "Morning. I'm Frank," he said, and stuck his hand out to Demme.

"Demetrius," Demme said, and they shook. Branhan worried about what Dad might say, but the gentleman in him didn't fail. While Branhan spread chicken salad on toasted bread, Demme only got the barest details of his life in before the old man started in on his rodeo days and the crazy-sounding reining circuit.

The man talked more to Demme than he'd said to Branhan in a month. Branhan had seen this before, back when they still went to church, when he was a boy and his mother was with them. Once, then, his father had driven out well before dawn to barbeque chicken for a fundraiser. He and a few men grilled hundreds of halved roasters on massive cookers. Around noon when folks came to pick them up, Frank did all the selling. The man didn't talk much in his daily life but when it came to something important, he knew how to make people feel welcome.

The three ate together at the kitchen table, passing plates to one another. Sweet tea, chips from the gas station, and chicken salad with pickles. Once, while Demme rinsed the dishes at the sink, Frank turned to him with a look of some kind of understanding. Whatever it was, there was a blessing to it. And Branhan knew, in that deep part of him, that there was so very much blessedness to it, to all of it.

Nightmares of Darkness and Heat

The pines by the house are one shadow and our van's headlights push the darkness far into the woods. It rushes back when they cut off. I know hell is not in that house.

The sun was setting when we left Delia. Waves of heavy cloud hung over us, so bright it looked like if they dropped they would incinerate us. I pointed them out to Ashley and she looked into the small glaring sun with me and said "Yeah, it's beautiful."

I tried to sit next to her in the van but she sat with the other girls. I listened to my music and watched the lit-up parking lots of Albany pass by.

Tommy, our youth director, acted like we all already knew what the house was so he didn't explain it. The others said it was about heaven and hell and people dying. Then you get Dairy Queen after.

In class we read that the woods are lovely, dark, and deep. The woods behind the house would be quiet—I can tell by looking. Besides, there wouldn't be a hundred laughing youth like there are here, and no blaring music. Maybe Ashley would go back there with me, just to hear the quiet. How do you ask a girl to do that?

Tommy gives us bright yellow wristbands and says, "Once you get your wristband, go on in and wait in the lobby." He adds, "Don't get Cokes or anything, you can't carry them through." Jim comes over to me. We've known each other since preschool. Jim spent the night at my house last weekend and we talked about girls. It took a long time for me to admit that I liked Ashley. He likes Brittany. Neither of us have ever asked a girl out.

Ashley wears sweaters with just her fingers poking out of the sleeves. She never sits at our lunch table and we never sit at hers because it's full of girls. Tommy sometimes talks about how lust is a sin and so is masturbation and the two go together because you're not thinking of like a tree when you do it. But with Ashley, I just wish her niceness was mine—or that she'd point it at me.

The house is old. Its paint peels in strips and its windows are the old kind with thick glass. I get the feeling like it's tired of having all these kids run through it. The windows upstairs are blacked out so you can't see in, but we hear people screaming up there.

Ashley told me she saw a ghost once at the church campground. The counselors took her group straight through this creepy ruined house, past the fallen staircase and out the back door. Ashley knew there were people waiting to jump out at them. Once they got outside, sure enough, a counselor in a black robe ran after them. Ashley knew it was coming so she didn't run. Instead she stayed and looked up at the window in the top floor, where she saw a white face disappear behind a curtain.

I like ghost stories but I can't get them out of my head. Like when I'm in that sleep where I'm awake but I can't move or scream, I see things in the corners of my room.

Inside the house, kids and their parents drink Cokes. There aren't enough seats for everyone so we camp out on the floor, which is warped like crazy. I sit by Jim. Ashley is in her group of girls. Jim says, "I went through one of these last year but it wasn't this big."

"Is it scary?"

"The hell part kind of is. It depends on how they do it."

I read the Bible and try to do the things Jesus says to do but a lot of it is about divorce and money and I'm not married. I don't have any money either. Tommy never talks about the parts I marked with a pencil—Jesus drinking wine or the demon-possessed guy they chained up. That's the stuff I'd like to hear about.

We're going in. The hall is dark and tall. There are those little windows above the doors. Our whispers echo.

The first scene has people standing in front of school lockers, talking. They aren't really talking, just moving their heads and looking around like they were talking. Two people in front are actually talking. One wants to go to a party and the other doesn't. The first guy gets louder, he really wants to go to this party, and the second one finally agrees, says okay. The second guy carries a Bible so I guess he's not supposed to be going to parties.

We move to the next scene. I hear Ashley's voice behind me. She talks too quickly for me to understand. The cluster of girls giggle. I wish I knew what they were talking about.

Once Dad and I went to a crazy lady's house. Dad told me she was our cousin and she went through phases of being really depressed and then really happy and now she was in the happy phase. She lived by herself and had piles of things everywhere: columns of magazines, stacks of kitchen utensils, rows of empty pots. Upstairs we came to her son's bedroom. She told us he shot himself in that room and what was weirder was how calmly she said it. Just like the rest of the house, that bedroom had neat piles of things everywhere. In fact there were *Playboy* magazines stacked on his bed. The top magazine's cover showed a big-haired woman with her arm across her boobs. The picture was faded it had sat there so long. I thought about taking it. I didn't, not because of lust or whatever, but because there was something sad and gross about it. By then the crazy lady and Dad had gone back downstairs and I was alone there where he'd shot himself.

I thought, later, when I was in bed almost asleep, that the boy's ghost might have come after me if I took the magazine.

The next scene is two girls at their school lunchroom. More people are in the back fake-talking. The girl tells her friend about being depressed. The depressed girl wears a lot of black, but you can tell it's not her usual thing. Her nails aren't painted black, either. The depressed girl's friend talks about how much God loves the depressed girl and has her Bible out. Shaking her head, the depressed girl leaves. There is no God, she says. Her friend stays and says a prayer, Help Jenny dear Lord, help Jenny find her way Lord.

She should have said There is no love.

Once Ashley wrote me a note. I don't understand how girls have such perfect handwriting when guys' handwriting looks like we're still in first grade. The note just said hi, asked about my classes and said how bored she was in hers. She drew a turtle beside where she put Your friend, Ashley. I wrote her one back and tried to fold it like she did hers.

That night I dreamed that my house was floating on the ocean and I was in the attic looking out through the windows.

I have nightmares many nights. When I was little, they were of something big and evil chasing me through the house. I tried to scream but couldn't. It chased me but I never saw what it was—I only knew it was big and it stank like when you find a dead thing in the woods and it wanted to kill me. Later I had the same dream but the big evil thing was different. Instead of being in one place, it buzzed the air in the attic and all through the house. I couldn't run or scream because it was in the house and there wasn't any getting away from it. I woke up those mornings, always Saturday mornings, and didn't move until I finally forgot the smell.

I have nightmares, too, where I see the shadows of demons coming down the hallway toward my bedroom. These nightmares, I know, are of my parents somehow. The demons scream and cackle and it is so, so loud.

Party scene. People dance and there's loud music. Everyone drinks from red plastic cups. It's kind of weird because they have all the lights on. Bible guy from earlier sips. He doesn't have his Bible anymore but he looks really uncomfortable. Why doesn't he just drink? Keri, one of our group, dances too and the girls giggle all over again. Bible guy wants to go home, he says. Other guy, who's pretending to be drunk, says fine, he'll drive, he's only had a few. Jim looks at all the people dancing in the back, particularly at one hot girl.

The first time I drank out of the bottles in the dining room it gave me a coughing fit. My stomach felt empty in a weird way but I didn't puke. I felt lighter and kind of happy. My parents keep other bottles in the desk, in the kitchen, all over the place. I found out the more you drink the less weird it gets. If you drink enough, you drift off past the spins to a place nightmares can't get to.

Tommy tells us not to drink.

The depressed girl is in her bedroom. There's a poster of a band with wild hair on the wall and her bed isn't made up. She has a bottle of pills, the red round type of bottle not the white, square kind. She cries and says There is no God no one can help me and she takes the pills. In like a second she slumps over and dies. I didn't see how many pills she took but you don't just keel over like that. She looked way too calm, too.

I've heard people at church say that suicide is the one unforgivable sin.

Maybe the whole thing about God is made up but I'm scared to think that.

Sometimes I feel something when I pray. Like God's presence with me.

Why is it so easy to feel like that thing from my nightmare is after me, but so hard to feel God?

Mawmaw says to pray for my angels to protect me. Tommy says God loves me and Jesus died for me and I am saved. Satan can't get me. I don't think Tommy knows much about the devil.

How can a short prayer save anybody when every night is so hard?

Mom's room is next to mine. I heard her crying in there with the door locked. I kept my eyes closed and prayed. Dad was out there so I couldn't go get a bottle.

We are quiet while the depressed girl dies. On the way to the next scene, the girls talk and I can tell Jim wants to talk about computer games or something but he won't right now.

The party guys have wrecked their car. Fake fire made from lights and streamers lick from the busted hood. Paramedics check their pulses and the drunk one is alive but Bible guy is dead. The paramedics don't yell or cry. They just check the pulse and lower their heads.

Ashley and the other girls' faces flash in the yellow ambulance lights. I have never seen them silent before. Ashley chews on her nails.

At the end of the hall Saint Peter is a fat man with a beard and a white acolyte robe. Ambulance lights flash on him and the dead girl and the dead guy, who stand before him. Saint Peter opens a big book and says, Yes, you knew Jesus, go on to your reward and Bible guy walks through a door on the right. You, however, never knew Jesus, and cannot go to heaven, he tells the girl. Someone in black, hunched over and wiry, runs through us. This thing runs and grabs her and pulls her through the door on the left. The door stands open, gaping into the dark.

We go in. Tommy says Put your hands on the shoulders of the person in front of you, and I put my hands on Jim's shoulders. Keri's hands are on mine. The way Tommy talks about it, God and Satan can look into your brain. They have seen what I've done, what I've thought.

We're in the room in the house. Heat burns my eyes. They've got it turned up so hot you can't breathe right. That depressed girl wails. We walk in a line in the dark and I hear her wailing. Is that what happens if you kill yourself? The girl screams, Why didn't I accept Jesus, and they're torturing her somehow. Other people scream too, but we can't see anything in the darkness.

Buzzing in the air, in the heat. It's the same feeling.

If I say I won't drink anymore, I won't think about girls, I'll read my Bible more and pray more—then will it stop hurting? Will God make it stop hurting?

Can you die from losing track of yourself? Like, wandering so far off in your mind you stay gone, separated?

It was the time I drank all the liquor I could and took a handful of pills from all the different bottles and drank my old expired cough syrup too and I lay there for a long time wanting to sleep without nightmares and be done. I kept drinking liquor because I knew I hadn't drank enough. I woke up the next day and thought I still might die. By Monday I went to school and spent lunch in the bathroom wanting to die.

Mom and Dad didn't notice because they were drunk too that night.

A new room. Light. Jesus is tall, bearded, and he smiles. Bible guy gets a hug and joins the angels. The angels are girls in bedsheets but lots of bedsheets. Jesus tells us that if we pray that same short prayer we will go to Heaven and be in Glory with Him. He says if we need to pray, there are ministers in the back.

There is silence. The room feels cool and empty.

I go to the back after a few others do and a minister with buzzed hair whose breath smells a little takes me to a corner and asks if I want to be in Heaven with Jesus when I die.

Yes, I tell him. He prays with me and I repeat what he says. The minister smiles and says angels are partying big time because in the Bible it says that the hosts of Heaven rejoice over one sinner that is saved. I tell him, I'm not saved. He smiles. You are if you say the prayer, he says. You can be sure of it.

But I need more saving. He asks what I mean.

My parents, they tell me we can't let it out around town. Dad is respected. At Mom's job, they couldn't have it. So when I break down without saying anything, the minister puts a hand on my shoulder and prays for everything except what it feels like I need.

The minister hugs me and his shirt is sweated through.

One of the retired preachers at church is short and stooped. He has to tilt his head up to look directly into my eyes, but when he does, I know he's really looking. I can't think of another adult with that much kindness in them—it's like a cloud of kindness around this man. During Wednesday Night Supper one week, he put his hand on my shoulder, tilted his head to see me, and smiled. I'm praying for you, he said.

I hope he keeps praying for me. Maybe his prayers will work.

There's no face in the window when I look back at the house. We go to Dairy Queen, and I sit away from everybody. My face hurts from trying not to cry. Jim sits with me but I don't talk and he doesn't either. The others talk and laugh and giggle.

I look out of the window on the van ride home. Once we leave the city the woods turn dark. Turning up my music is like going away inside myself, only the nightmares are there, waiting. Every shadow I see looks like one. And where I'm going it's only more darkness, more heat, and being alone.

Who will save me?

Gone Cold
and Black and Blue

They hadn't even opened the bottle of Seghesio Alan had bought for the party when the damn ghost started up again. This time it was footsteps in the upstairs hallway, Alan gazing at the ceiling as though footprints might press through the sheetrock. Beth Shea drew deep breaths, perhaps ready to run again. Jack said, obvious after four glasses, "We better check it out." Then he didn't move. Alan's wife, Lorene, did not look up from the plate of cheese she sliced with a paring knife. Everyone knew she preferred to ignore, or perhaps leave alone, whatever it was that haunted the house.

Alan grabbed a flashlight. "I'll go with you," Benny said. The foyer was dark except for a little decorative table lamp that threw yellow light between the posts of the banister. Alan held the flashlight against his shoulder like a cop. It was not an aggressive attitude, but the ready caution with which Alan faced the unknown. He and Benny climbed one stair at a time, peeking up from the landing.

Alan sighed. "Never a damn thing when you want it to be." Nothing moved in the hallway.

Benny said, "It's there. We just can't see it. Did you call those investigators I told you about?" Benny asked.

"What are they going to do?" Alan asked. "It would be a waste."

"They do it for free. You could get pictures, recordings, all sorts of things."

"Would they make it leave?"

"They're more into documentation."

Alan and Benny gazed down the hall, where the flashlight cast a tunnel of light. "They should've told me it was here when they sold me the house."

"You're the one who wanted an antebellum Georgian. It's got a widow's walk. You practically asked for it."

Alan grunted. They went back to the kitchen.

"See anything?" asked Beth Shea.

"No."

Lorene turned to them with full glasses. "Cheers," she said.

"Cheers," they said.

There wasn't much air behind Beth Shea's voice when she said, "Have you thought about asking a priest to remove it?"

"Do they charge?"

"Hell, they might give you two-fers." Jack said. "Maybe they use an undead fumigator."

Lorene said, "You can't get rid of something that isn't there."

Alan swilled his glass.

Over the next several weeks Alan worked on his novel, a family saga centered on the Kentucky town where he grew up. Lorene sat out on the back porch, leaving her papers and summer reading to collect dust in the office. Jack traveled to the everglades doing research for his new book. Beth Shea finally went on a retreat to a monastery in Virginia she'd talked about all year.

Once they all got back to Georgia, their parties resumed. A few lights flickered and doors creaked open far back in the house, but nothing happened that seemed more remarkable than what they'd seen already. Jack, without telling Alan, researched the house and property, finding out about the families who used to live there. He didn't dig far before he unearthed several culprits for the haunting: infants dead from typhoid, the mysterious disappearance of a female slave, one son whose birthday was six months after his older brother's and who moved to Boston as a young man. The whole thing reminded him of a Faulkner novel. Jack counted five possible entities, not counting any connected with the Muskogee tribes that used to live along the river, or Civil War soldiers wandering over from Andersonville. But the ghost had never appeared as a Confederate, a slave, or a Victorian invalid. Instead, it was all bumps and flashes; something exerting itself out of silence.

Alan laughed off these explanations. "My house has a ghost, so what?" he said. Nonetheless, one day Jack said to Benny, "Why wait until he gives the okay to investigate?"

"Because it's his house."

"Wouldn't you expect your friends to document your haunted house?"

"I wouldn't be opposed to it in the first place."

"Exactly. It's what he should want us to do."

So while Alan sat writing a stormy scene in which the mother finally reveals the death of a younger brother, Benny's SUV pulled up, filled with hardshell plastic cases. He and Jack grabbed two handfuls each, bringing it all inside as Alan drew his scene dark with storm clouds and tin-roof rain. They mounted infrared cameras and plugged in surge protectors full of power cords as Alan hinted the mother's memory toward a sick shape in the bed. They powered up electromagnetic field meters, high-fidelity audio recorders, and a very expensive thermal camera as Alan sized up his paragraph. Benny and Jack grinned. As Alan stared at the wall to let his mind formulate its next image into language, he heard a high electric whine and knew his house had been invaded. Or perhaps he knew by feel that they were there.

The downstairs looked like a movie set with all the wires. Alan said, "What have you made here?"

"We're committed now. This shit wasn't cheap to rent," Jack said.

"Give us twenty-four hours," Benny said, "Only one day and we'll see what we can find."

Alan stared from Jack, to Benny, to the humming contraptions surrounding them. "You bastards," he said. He smiled in spite of himself.

"Alan, we're your friends," Jack said, "And this is what friends do: thoroughly investigate your haunted house with expensive equipment so we can put the evidence on the Internet."

"Fine," he said, "Just don't put anything on the antiques. And don't nail anything in." He went back to writing with new momentum.

All that day, Benny and Jack spread A/V equipment through the house until no room was spared. Alan climbed his stairs to face a camera and tripod down the hallway. His hands in the kitchen sink were closely monitored since the ghost had once turned the faucet on and off. He heard Benny talking to people on the phone, asking about each piece of equipment and detailing the "incidents" they had seen. It wouldn't be long before the investigators recruited Benny, Alan thought. Maybe Rhetoric and Composition was so boring that hunting ghosts seemed like a solid career change.

"We might actually get evidence," Benny said. "We could come one step closer to knowing whether these things are really beings from another spiritual state, or left over emotional energy, or wandering electromagnetic fields—you know, that's one theory: when the field comes into contact with a human, it throws off synapses in the brain and causes hallucinations. Some people theorize that the fields are sentient, that they can manipulate the effect so that the person sees exactly the thing that he or she—"

"Will they pay us for it?"

Gravel crunched in the drive. The men looked at one another. Alan went to the door to try and intercept Lorene before she saw everything, but there was no missing the "control room" Benny and Jack had colonized in the front parlor.

Lorene stopped in the open doorway. Alan leaned in beside her. "They set it up before I could say anything. Benny said it would only be for tonight, then they'll pack it up."

"Is this all about that thing?"

"Yeah." He glanced over three computer monitors. "If they can't find it with this, nobody can."

"It's a waste. How much did they pay for all of it?"

"It's rented," Jack said.

She snorted. Contemptuous, but a laugh. Alan wished he could see her eyes behind the sunglasses. She walked past him. Later, when Alan walked upstairs, he found the micro-recorders and cameras that had been in their bedroom piled in the hallway. He already knew the door was locked.

"Okay, time to sit back and see what happens." Benny clinked his glass with the others'. "Here's to Hamlet's daddy."

Benny, Jack, Alan, and Lorene sat in folding chairs. Large monitors rested on a moving quilt laid over Alan's antique spruce coffee table. One screen showed the hallway in grayscale. Other rooms were only occupied by blinking recorder lights. The heavy grandfather in the hall tocked. Nothing creaked.

"So this is what you do," Lorene said, "You get all this stuff and run it all over the place and you stare at it."

"It's an experiment. Can't you imagine actually seeing something? Even just a movement, caught on film, able to be analyzed," Benny said.

"I don't see a thing moving. Can't we play some music?"

"Not with the recorders. It would cause interference."

"This whole thing is an interference."

"Just one night, Lorene, that's all," Alan said.

"One night too long. Wait, look! No, sorry, that was a glare from outside."

They all jumped toward the monitor then settled back. Silence for a while. Sips, shifting seats. The high whine of empty rooms. Alan wondered how many glasses Lorene had had before they sat down to watch. Her face in the gray-blue monitor light was old. Her still eyes reflected it as though they had no color of their own. Alan could barely see the woman who spent their whole first summer with him in a cabin without electricity, where they pumped clean water from a well and spent half their nights on a blanket on the screened-in porch, moving out of reach of the mosquitoes and all the rest of the world. Only twenty years.

Benny's phone rang. The conversation was short. He flipped it shut and said, "Beth's on her way."

They stared at him. "Beth Shea wants to be a part of this?" Lorene asked.

"Yeah," Benny said, watching the monitor, "She says she wants to face her fears. How about a few passes before she gets here?"

"Yes, thank God," said Jack.

"All right, you first then. Grab one of the infrareds."

"Got it."

Jack lifted the camera, turning its viewfinder to face him. He finished his wine and climbed the stairs. In only a few minutes, Jack returned and laid the camera on the moving quilt and went to the kitchen. "Well?" Lorene asked.

"Did you pick up anything?" Benny said.

Jack poured a glass of Scotch and stood. "Yeah. There was something."

Benny's eyes grew huge. "Did you get a good image? What about audio, did you ask it anything?"

"You want to talk to it?" Lorene asked. Alan heard a slur beginning in her voice. He knew better than to place a hand on her arm to calm her.

"Usually EVP's occur when an investigator engages the entity. Whatever these things are, they understand speech," Benny said. Then he bent his head again in thought, parsing out a thesis on the contexts of discourse between the living and the dead. "I'll take my turn now, then," Benny said, and climbed the stairs wrapped in equipment.

The couple sat in silence. From the corner of his eye, Alan watched Lorene's leg jog up and down. He felt the need to calm her down, but before he came up with a plan, she asked, "Are you all done yet?"

"Remember, we agreed to let them do this for the night, babe," Alan said.

"Don't talk to me like I'm a dog. I didn't say anything about it, and there's cameras in my bathroom. Are you looking for a shit ghost?"

Benny came down. He didn't look at Lorene. "Your turn if you want to go up, Alan."

"What am I supposed to do?"

"Take the thermal camera up there and walk around, see if you find anything. We've done a good infrared sweep but we haven't run the thermal." Benny lifted the heavy apparatus into

Alan's arms. "You might try your bedroom, it's all that's left un-less somebody's tackling the attic."

"Sure to God you're not taping the bedroom with that stuff," Lorene said.

"It's just for a minute, babe." He waved the thermal camera toward her. Waves of heat in the shape of a woman. "Only a min-ute, and we'll be done."

Lorene stood, flung the door open, and left for the porch. Her chair flew back, nearly upsetting several glasses on a table. Benny said with gentleness, "You go, Alan, I'll clean this up."

Everything was dark, but Alan could see altogether differ-ently in the thermal camera. The stairs and hallway were blue with cool. All the lines and corners rounded—only color was left. Heat, warmth, cold.

Bedroom door—he paused by the knob. Would it be there, when he opened the door? Had it been there the whole time, and left? One red splotch of warmth . . . or cold, Benny said they were. Alan opened the door. Blue, green. Yellow coming in the window, or maybe it was blue getting out because the old things weren't well insulated. Ceiling fan whirred azure.

Bed: all blue, blue, blue. No warmth by the pillows nor in the creases from their sleeping. Near black at the vent. All black; only in the camera did that unfalsified world of color appear. Can't fake warmth—hot or cold, warm. All things hued.

Dresser. Pictures: his father in Mexico, negative-like. Barely make it out. Probably can tell only because he knows that shape, that image. Lorene . . . smile clear as day, Cheshire against the muddled blue inarguables. Change? Sure, but only along one scale, from hot to cold—easy to tell. She was hot downstairs—didn't look at her with it long—it would make her angry— would resentment pick up? No, and he didn't need it. Near black by the wine glass, gone blue and green like a northern sea off Ireland or Maine where it looks like charred steel. Everything black by the vent.

Alan switched off the thermal and sat on the edge of the bed. He didn't realize how much the camera illuminated. Cold dark without it. Bed blue beneath him, although it didn't look it, didn't glow. But it was blue growing into red where he sat, he knew. Eyes adjusted. Everything half shadow half imagined, his brain filling in the vacancies, imagining boundaries that could hold in reality. Untrustworthy, his eyes. Not exact as the camera. Eyes to see a thing and miss all of its properties, or else misinterpret them—maybe the mind was the culprit, as he saw objectively and changed the image to fit his beliefs, eliminating features and adding phantom characteristics, all in swift clicking synapses between eyeball and brain. Cheshire smile—one hell of an interpretation.

Alan sat a while before he pulled the recorder from his pocket. Flicked it on and turned the red light away from him. In a dark, dark house, the story went. Chuckled. "What is your name?" Listen . . . no answer: but don't they show up even if you don't hear anything? How long to wait? Like students in class. *In a dark, dark room in a dark, dark house.* "Why are you here? Are there more than one of you?" Well . . . "are" refers to the "more than one," or even just "more," so it would be plural . . . "Why do you stay here?" *In a dark, dark chest in a dark, dark room in a dark, dark house.* She didn't want to record in the bedroom.

Alan shifted. *Dark, dark box in the dark, dark chest . . .* "Is my wife really scared of you?" Red bed, red with heat from where he sat. Jack had come down pale and reaching for the Balvenie. *In that dark, dark box, there was . . .* "What happened to us?" He sat there a long while and carried the camera down without turning it on again.

Downstairs, he tossed the recorder down. Beth Shea walked in from the kitchen. She wore a rosary.

"Are you sure about this?" Alan asked her.

She smiled, stretching her lips to cover nervousness, but she held herself in a way Alan hadn't seen before. "I am. I've thought about it and talked to some very wise people and I think it will be a good thing."

Benny handed her an old camera. "We haven't taken any stills. I saved the mechanical for you. Activity tends to screw up digitals, but there's no wiring in that thing at all."

Beth took the camera and walked slowly, deliberately up the stairs.

Alan saw Lorene's silhouette through the blue monitor's reflection. The French door was ajar, bending all its reflections so that the house fell in on itself. He opened the door.

Lorene was a ringing shadow against the moon-streaked lake, buzzing like the July air itself. She felt him behind her. She had been waiting. Let him see my face. She turned. Scowled. And him with that over-the-glasses look, obsequious. That's one word for it.

Alan said, "I didn't see anything." Then, "I didn't record very long."

Doesn't change the fact you did. "What are you going to do if they find something? Live here with some dead bastard watching you when you sleep?" Selfish is what it was, selfishness. Didn't ask her whether to turn her house into a horror movie set. For nothing—there never was anything, just Beth Shea's hysterics and men wanting hobbies, men needing something to do with themselves. He knew exactly how much she hated it, and did it anyway.

Alan looked at her and saw her face pale and hollowed from the moonlight behind her. Beauty, it once had. Beauty still, but angry and . . . pickled. The humid night did not press on him harder than the look she gave him, sunk as it was—the part of her he loved seemed to drown in it. He was sober and could see it without any infidelity. "Lorene, it's only for tonight, then they'll be gone. Just one night. If you want, tomorrow we can go out to Daphne's. We don't even have to talk about this anymore."

"You know how those two are. They'll be on this for a solid month—until classes start back and they actually have to work. And you'll follow right along with them."

Moonlight caught her iris— her left iris alone, not the white—and light fell softly on her face so that the only shining thing was the iris, slim as a wedding band and shining cold. All else haze, near black. What happened? Months before—in the semester? Busy with finals, might not have said or done enough—when did she start drinking badly? Parties—then the two of them—then herself alone. Had the scale gone to black without him knowing?

Alan turned and went inside.

Jack was in the kitchen. Every single light down to the oven's and microwave's was turned on and he sat with his back to the windows. "They find anything else?" he asked.

"Don't know yet. Beth Shea, maybe." Alan sat.

"We should have left it alone."

"I wish we would've. But it wouldn't leave us alone either."

"How's Lorene with it?"

"Not very good."

"She might understand it better than the rest of us. How it's one of those things you don't mess with."

"No. For her, it's not even there anymore."

New tumbler, two neat.

"Or it's there too much," Jack said. "Alan, are you two all right?"

Later, Benny called and everyone gathered around the screens. "We didn't do too bad considering it's one night and we're all amateurs. First, here's Jack's."

A grainy grayscale video played, jumping around, in which a vague shadow hovered. Benny looped it. "That could be a reflection from the doorway there. I meant to tell him to close all the doors before he started." Next, he pulled up a spiked line graph. "This is mine. Nothing spectacular, but a high EMF reading that came and went in the bathroom. It's hard to say if it was something in the house since I didn't check where the air conditioning ducts were, or maybe ballasts for the—"

"Okay, come on Benny," said Jack.

Benny shuffled some things on the table. "Final thing, at least until we develop Beth Shea's film, is an EVP that Alan picked up."

"I did?" It was the same feeling as seeing a letter from a prospective publisher.

Benny played an audio file. Alan heard himself, wearier than he remembered, saying "What happened to us?" Then a gust of static shaped into consonants.

"That was it?" Jack asked. "That's what you were looking for?"

"Shh. Listen again."

Everyone leaned forward. Alan: "What happened to us?" Ghost: crackle of language.

"'Your head's on my bed?'" Jack said.

"'I said what I said?'" Beth Shea offered.

"No, there are three 'd' sounds. Could be a muffled 't.'"

"You know this is bullshit, don't you?" Jack said.

"Inaccurate and hard to understand, yes, but even if it's just radio interference, it's saying something in English. Alan, do you have any ideas? You were up there with it."

"No. Can't tell," he told them. But he knew what it said. He went to the porch.

The bottle was with Lorene, set on the deck chair alongside her. Her glass was shattered against the opposite rail. Alan called to her.

She turned, hair askance—a bubbling of fumes into her brain and her personality set firmly on bitch. Which he loved her for sober and happy. Make fun, take no shit, push him down in bed *my head's on your bed*. But not like this. Didn't her iris gleam?

"Get them the hell out."

"They're your friends, Lorene."

"Not with all this hocus pocus."

Maybe not so far gone—maybe ready to talk—Jesus, months of her on the porch with wine. Of her late awake and him never falling asleep with her. Of her turning to face the wall. *My head, your bed, I said.* Months. Why hadn't they talked?

"Lorene, I'm sorry. I shouldn't have let them do this. I didn't know it would—"

"Don't." Turned to face the lake, her hand on the armrest by the table with the wine had nails chipped from picking. Why hadn't he noticed before? *I said, I said.* Black by the vent. And here my wife, already buried under July cicadadrone. Had he been the shovel? *The dead . . .* His stomach dropped like it hadn't since his own mother died, since that phone call rang outside of time (they show up even if you don't hear anything). He had heard nothing in that static babble. His wife was only drunk. In the morning—in light—there would be no creaking stairs nor shadow to stand in his hall and tell him which and how. No, damn them, his life, his wife.

She stirred. Face streaked and shadowed and glowing. "I'm so sorry," he told her. "I don't want us to be like this."

She looked, and several spirits shifted across her.

"You made us like this."

"I didn't know—"

"You'll go looking for this ghost but you're just now interested in us?"

"I didn't—"

"Then you're blind. You're dead yourself. We're dead."

"We don't have to be."

"Did you forget?"

Forgot—Oh God—the one who died—

Lorene glared at him, reading him, and said, "You did. You're only the father, of course you did. We're all dead. At least I've chosen my grave—" she shook the wine bottle— "What's yours?"

Alan couldn't believe he didn't think of it, that season not even of death, it felt, but of life that never came. He'd wandered through that time, no clue how to comfort her, and now the ghost—that insistence that they were no longer by themselves in some way. "Can we talk about this tomorrow?" he asked. Shame and despair ran through him, and a deep desire to drink.

Lorene turned away, face to the wall.

Alan turned to go inside, her silence behind him echoing the phrase: *the dead find the dead.*

All three of them had been watching him. "Beth Shea," Alan said, "Can you get it out?"

"I think so. They told me how to do it."

"Do it. Please."

As she climbed the stairs, Alan went to the kitchen to drink with Jack.

The only thing Benny sent to the South Georgia Paranormal Research Society was a still photo that Beth Shea had taken on the widow's walk. In it, a pale candleflame figure hovered just above the roof boards, the lake shimmering behind it. She had been right when she explained what she saw; it was beautiful.

There are no graves for some deaths. Alan drove Lorene to the graveyard of a Baptist church down the road where the generations petered out from the ancient mossy stones to the brilliant new ones. The couple walked among them, spotting infant graves with little marble footstones. They were silent as the wind blew the scent of honeysuckle over them. When Lorene sat before a stone chiseled with the image of a lamb, Alan joined her on the ground. They did not speak, and touched very little, just Alan's hand on Lorene's shoulderblade. The stone was so white he could barely read the inscription. The date of death was 1925.

After a long while they rose. The two continued, broken, but together.

Why Can't You Be True

Mabby and Jennifer eased three black widow spiders out of the corner of the steel boat before they got in, oaring through cobwebs to clamp in the battery. They slid the boat over the bank's coarse tawny sand into the lake where it bobbed in a gentle wake. Mabby stood barefoot in the water, holding the boat steady as Jennifer climbed in from shore. Trolling upriver through wisps of fog, they stopped seeing houses and saw snakes and alligators then nothing at all but tangles on the banks. Mabby muttered, perhaps to herself, "I imagine this is the place of the horned god."

Jennifer's coffee began to kick in. "That name always sounded strange to me. Does it sound strange to you?"

Mabby thought. She gazed into the white cedar boughs then into the scrub below. She said, "All of it sounds strange. I think that's because it's true." She said to her new friend, "Would you like to hear how I got started with the craft?"

There were rumors of her floating around school, that girl who cast spells. They said she worshipped the devil or was possessed, that she didn't shave or shower. That she didn't like men. When I finally found her, Delilah wasn't the one I expected.

Maybe I thought she'd wear all black and have bars through her nose. Instead, Delilah was short and only wore some black. The beauty she had came from and reflected her joy. The only outward sign of her belief was the triple moon tattoo across her upper back, which disappeared after the dress code changed—but that was later.

I was worried to talk to her about something the other girls only whispered about. Maybe I sought her out because I was lonely. But I did have an intense desire to learn the craft. My soul was drawn to it like it was something I might have loved in a past life. People get those feelings sometimes.

Finally, one day I was in the library—if I finished my classwork I always asked to go to the library. Delilah walked in and pulled some black-bound book off a shelf and sat reading. It was just we two and the librarian at her computer. I knew the time had come. My knees shook as I walked by her and whispered, "I want to know about what you do."

Delilah turned as though she knew me, as though she'd been waiting for me to speak to her. She said, "Which thing? I throw pottery, write poetry, play guitar . . . "

"I want to know about being a witch."

She grinned like we both knew a secret. "Blessed be," she said.

Beginning that day, and through many hours at the library, we read books about the Goddess and the rituals. We giggled at the pictures of skyclad practitioners. We studied with some fear the images of the gods and goddesses—those drawings and carvings were ancient, signifying things that had mattered to humanity for thousands of years, hundreds of generations.

Along with the study of Wicca came the study of feminism. We nearly memorized the three feminist books in the library. I stopped shaving and wearing makeup. People had that part right about us, but we did shower so I don't know where they dug up that rumor. Probably the sight of arm hair made them think we were filthy. My Aunt Tabitha, whom I lived with then as now, didn't mind any of it since she was an old hippie herself. But I didn't tell her about Wicca until later.

Two more girls joined our coven, both of them graduated but still around. One wore no makeup, the other had liner in catlike arches around her eyes.

My first-ever ritual was at Delilah's house. I stumbled through the prayers, beet-faced, trying to keep up with the order of things. In a steam of incense, it was over and we drank Delilah's mother's sweet tea and sat in lawn chairs on her back porch, watching the traffic roll through town.

Delilah asked me, "What did you think?"

"It was weird," I said. "But it was beautiful."

Delilah smiled. "I know."

She took me to my first party out at the lake. Under an old pavilion surrounded by pines and live oaks and Spanish moss wafting in the wind, a jam band played. Cold beer cans floated through the crowd. We found the coolers before too long. Girls spun in hippie skirts. One young mother danced with her dreadlocked husband, their cherub child on his shoulders. Boys at the edges of the yellow stage lights appeared and fell to shadow, until I saw the one I wanted and snaked my arms through the crowd, shifting to the beat to get to him. I may not have known witchcraft, but I knew how to dance. We danced until sweat shone on Delilah's tattoo, those moons reflecting the heavy quarter moon above it all.

Late that night, couples found corners of the wide lot and curled up. My boy and I kissed, we held one another just like the warm, humid air around us held our bodies. We lay there until the bugs came with a vengeance, driving us into his car. By then it was very late. He lay back and snored, but I couldn't sleep. I didn't want that night to get away. I walked down the embankment to the blue hole, a deep place. Pine needles reached for me. I slipped into the almost-warm water. Felt it cover me. I swam a while, watched the moon set, felt the others fall asleep, and thought about this new world I had come into.

But that moon did set. It didn't take long for the whole school, including the meanest of them, boys and girls, to learn that I had joined Delilah in her witchcraft. That's what they called it, no matter what we said. Notes appeared in my locker: some were nice about the love of Jesus, and others were furious about the fires of hell. Girls who carried Bibles with their books stopped by mine and Delilah's table during lunch, talking about God loving us as though we had abused that love or abused God. I was afraid of them.

"They talk about us in Sunday school, at church," Delilah told me. "Their leaders tell them that they can love their God more by telling us about him. They're terrified to do it."

"Why can't they just leave us alone? Don't they know we don't care about anything they have to say?"

Delilah leaned close to me. We were in the library and I'd gotten too loud. Delilah said, "We can't be angry with them, Mab. I know it's shitty. Some of them are shitty. But we're the minority here. It wasn't that long ago that their people were burning our people alive."

"So we have to smile and listen to them tell us God hates us?"

"You know none of the Gods or Goddesses hate you." Delilah took a deep breath and said, "I believe that under everything, even these jerks, runs the energy of the Goddess, and that energy is love. It's love, not a fight, that gets the blessing of the universe."

Delilah talked to the Christians who came to us. When they got out their Bibles, she listened patiently. Most of the time she got them talking about something altogether different, something normal like playing volleyball or the latest horror movie. They expected us to snarl and hate them. Our kindness was a surprise. Delilah had been right in that.

I won't say I wasn't ever enchanted by them. One night music floated to me along the clay road as I walked and when I sat with my back to the rear wall of the church, I could feel the harmony through the boards. They were the type of church that sang without instruments. I didn't want to admit that the place was holy. Maybe it was holy because of their voices.

Walking back, I wondered how something so beautiful could be wrapped up with the fear of those girls at our lunch table, or in the hate-dripping hell notes that showed up in my locker.

I asked Delilah if there were any songs about the Goddess. One of her books included lyrics but no music. We pieced a song together with one of her friends from a band. Allison, one of the coven who had grown up going to church, joined in with a harmony. While we sang, I felt disembodied, never closer to oneness with the others and with the Goddess. Never more like myself. We all smiled at one another as we sang, amazed at what was happening—it, too, was holy. We had made, or done, something holy. We had loosed it into our lives and into the world.

Delilah had plans to get out of Delia. We all did around graduation time, but she was serious about it. The colleges she applied for, all of which accepted her, were in Colorado, New Mexico, California, and Boston. All at least four states away. I congratulated her on each new acceptance letter. I helped her hang maps of the Rockies in her bedroom. Meanwhile the applications the guidance counselor had given me gathered dust on the table where Aunt T leaves her keys everyday.

Delilah left for Boulder. I wrote her letters every week, sometimes sent pencil sketches of lake trees. She wrote back and we talked about funny things from a few years before, about what Boulder was like. Her new coven. She sketched pictures of the mountains. Soon I couldn't recall, exactly, what her face looked like without looking at pictures.

We were so close before she left that people at school called us lesbians. In a bitter phase, I theorized that the Christians became bored calling us witches so they found a new name. But just like Wicca is a different way of being in the world, what Delilah and I were was different from any of their names for it.

Delilah wrote back steadily for a while, then less and less. The first Christmas she sent a blue-glazed chalice she had turned in ceramics class. I sent her a painting of a magnolia bloom and my best poem. When the letters grew scarce, I didn't demand more. Delilah was in the next part of her life, while I remained here, and that became all right. My blood needs this heat too much to live in snowy Boulder.

Later, after high school was over and my friends scattered, I got in my Aunt's canoe and paddled north, along this same channel. I stayed as long as I could in that place of the horned god before I turned around and paddled back feeling grim. Tabitha never knew I was gone. That was the first of my wanderings.

I wandered, meeting the people of the lake, those who live in odd cabins or on boats or nowhere at all. The workers who set buoys and run the dam, the golf-course rednecks, the real rednecks. Occasionally I would talk about the craft, but when I asked if they knew any Wiccans, people raised their eyebrows. A few started to tell me about Jesus before I turned my back on them.

I stopped riding in cars or wearing shoes. There were enough dirt roads around the lake and enough people I knew who owned boats that I could go anywhere I wanted to. I almost stopped needing people, in terms of friends, although no one can ever completely stop that.

Then one day, after months of wandering, I came back. I remember it: the dirt road hummed with insects I used to know the names of. They were voices out of time, the same as they were when I was young and the same as they would be when I was old. With vines grown over the road banks, there was nothing along that path except the path itself that suggested humanity. Loneliness lay over me like the heat and like death. Inevitable loneliness. In the Goddess I was connected to all things: the trees, the honeysuckle I could smell but not see, the blackberries and milkweeds. But I didn't feel connected. I felt like I could dissipate into that heat, melt like the witch everyone told me I was and disappear. It would be neither good nor bad, neither painful nor pleasurable; just a gentle stretching and I'm daydreaming without wake.

I touched my forehead. Sweat dripped cool and sharp into the corners of my eyes. I felt my shoulders and they too had a water-covering shining on them. I lifted my arms and a faint breeze sifted through my hair, just enough to run across my back, and I knew I was alive.

The road came out at the boat club property. A swarthy old power company worker was taking a nap in the back of his truck, snoring. I took the paper wrapper from his lunch, folded it into a crane, and left it perched on his chest for him to figure out when he woke up.

When I got home, I tried looking up my old coven. It felt like being a girl again, asking parents listed in the phone book where my friends were. Allison had moved to North Carolina. I didn't know Meredith's last name and couldn't find it out to find her. I asked Delilah in a letter but she didn't know either.

I prepared to practice alone if I had to. Then another letter came from Delilah. She had talked to a friend in a coven up in Athens and found out about another Wiccan across the lake. Below this news, Delilah wrote a phone number and the name: Lilith.

The voice on the phone held back secrets, letting me know that I would never know. She asked me to meet her at an old church pavilion around the blue hole. I knew the place. It was where all the alligators stayed that got into the main lake, where no one would bother them.

Lilith, of course, was her craft name. She kept her real one a secret. Her blue eyes always seemed a little narrowed.

"Have you practiced before?" Lilith asked.

"All through high school with my friend Delilah and two others."

"How did you learn?"

"Delilah had some books. We got others from the library."

"It's dangerous to teach yourself. You should have found an experienced witch."

One thing that wandering does is make one wary of should. I said, "We knew the rede. We never did anything but blessings."

"There are dangers you couldn't have anticipated."

We had our first ritual at Lilith's house, that place stacked high with books that always seemed ready to fall on us. A many-windowed room was set up as a ritual space with deep red carpet, candles, and shelves upon shelves of oils, herbs, and trinkets. I hadn't seen anything like it. Anne, one of the coven, had the kindest expression I have ever seen. I was surprised at how old she was to be hanging around with us. Her Australian accent was cool too. There was a second woman dressed fully in black like a stereotypical Wiccan, who was quiet through the evening.

Short introductions and we began. Lilith spoke, her soft voice deepened to be clearer and—I guess sensual is what she was going for, like a poetry reading. With a silver chalice much nicer than the ceramic ones Delilah turned, she invoked the four winds and then the Goddess. When I heard that name from her lips it was like something I had never known before, even though I had known the Goddess, had felt the Goddess, experienced moments when I must have been one with the Goddess—but when Lilith said it, the name sounded like something I did not deserve.

The ritual was the same way. Familiar in its rhythm, yet packed with more words, finer incense, and a real and wicked-looking dagger on the altar. Not like the one Delilah and I got from a flea market. My consolation was seeing Anne immersed in the ritual, a contented smile on her face as she went through the parts and the motions with her eyes shut.

Lilith moved as though any ritual had to be done to an exact standard. When Delilah and I did ours together they ran with love, maybe they were a little scattered. How I liked it done. How it made sense. What I'm saying is that if we wanted some distant and disapproving god, we'd go to the meanest of the Bible churches and be content.

I caught myself beginning to hate Lilith when I hardly knew her.

Once it was over, Anne gave me a big hug and said I was welcome at her house anytime. She lived just off of the highway, over the bridge. Lilith showed me out with great courtesy and little warmth. The girl in black left early.

One of the friends I made during my wanderings was the pastor of the church near our house. I had been strolling through the graveyard that runs from the back door of the church into the woods when he came out to ask if I'd like a glass of water. It put me on guard—this tactic was a well-tried one from the Christians: they offered kindness as bait for a conversion talk. But it was very hot that day and I decided I could put up with some light preaching if it meant air conditioning and cold water. The pastor was young, not much older than me. His name was Kyle. He asked about me, my folks. I kept waiting for the sermon to begin but he only made conversation, gazing at me perhaps with confusion at the defensive hostility right below my surface. Somehow I started talking. I told Kyle about how other

Christians treated me, about how Delilah could talk them down from proselytizing.

"It was like they couldn't stand for us to be different," I said.

"Everybody needs a devil to disagree with," the young pastor said.

At some point in my descriptions of the rituals, maybe on the finer points of Wiccan god-in-all-being, Kyle became lost, outside his depth. He gave what I heard as an uncomfortable chuckle and said, "I don't know what makes you think I can help you with your Wicca problems. I can barely help people with their Christian ones."

"I want to get back to my practice, but she's—"

"Not Delilah?"

"Nowhere close. But I guess I knew it would be like that."

Kyle shifted. I suppose at some point he realized that he was alone in his church with a woman only slightly younger than he, who was also a witch. He said, "Give her a chance. If you don't like her group, maybe you could find another in Vienna or Americus."

"I don't have a car to get there."

"Then maybe you should get a job too."

I balled up one of his bulletins and threw it at him.

As I explained Wicca to the pastor, I came to understand it more myself. The craft was beautiful. That was why we did it and probably why the ancients did it, because it was a beautiful ordering of the world. A God and a Goddess, all things flowing into them and making them up, each person a part of them. In the ugliness of the world, we who were willing to call ourselves witches turned to the thing that was not only beautiful in itself, but that called us beautiful. Other faiths have nothing for women. Only the craft gave us a woman divinity.

And so many hated it for that. Perhaps in some deep place those people remembered the taste of the pyre's smoke in their lungs.

But it was also about power. We blessed knowing that we could curse even if it would destroy us. We bound together knowing we could tear apart. We healed knowing we could plague. The pastor was quiet after I told him that.

A clearing came into sight along the bank ahead of their boat, with a green lawn stretching almost to the water and bordered by a levy of planks. A few yards ashore, flowers of all colors bloomed in black plastic pots or in beds or on tables. A long greenhouse with a creaking, spinning fan stood beside the wide palette of flower colors. One turquoise shack with white-trimmed windows stood behind it all. The image of the whole place, forming as it did out of the primordial swamp, was of some sort of fantastical waystation.

Mabby turned the boat in and ran the bow onto a sandy bank. She and Jennifer climbed out, feeling the dew on their toes as they crossed the soft grass. For a few minutes they walked among the flowers, smelling the sweet blooms.

"These will make Big John's dock look like a paradise."

"That isn't easy."

A dark man with a ponytail came out to them, asking could he help them. He glanced at the empty parking lot. Mabby said, "We came by boat."

"Oh," the man said. He gave the impression that he wasn't very used to nor did he feel comfortable talking to people.

Soon the man wandered off, leaving Jennifer and Mabby to peruse, debating colors and combinations to hang on the bar's railings and posts. Bees hung over a bush of blue sage. The women knew they'd have to clean all the dead mayflies from the dock first, but their paired imaginations moved past the surface grime of Big John's, crafting between them the potential it may have for beauty. The selection of flowers they set aside on the green lawn was a brilliant, odd mix.

"We still have to pay," Jennifer said.

"How much do you have?"

The two women counted out their cash. It wasn't much. Mabby looked toward the shack where the shy clerk waited for them. She tugged down the front of her shirt and walked up to the cash register, pulling Jennifer with her. "Did you get all that rung up?" Mabby asked, leaning over the table.

"Yes ma'am, it comes to—"

"My friend's getting married. I told her it was more fun not to, but she really likes her Joe. Good for her, I guess, but I don't know how you can only love one person for always, when there's so many out there. What do you think?"

He glanced from the cash register to Mabby's chest to her eyes. She smiled at him. "That is true, there are a lot of people out there."

"Lots of people, and lots of them cute."

"Lots of them."

They left with those flowers for half price, holding back laughter as they loaded it all into the boat. The deck sank a few inches under the extra weight, and the little electric engine could barely push them. Mabby and Jennifer sat at either end of the craft, separated by such a large bouquet they looked like some Romantic painting. Once they found the channel again, Mabby continued.

During my wandering time, I fell for a man still tanned from the Iraqi sun. His name was Jimmy, or James, depending. It was his ever-deep eyes, the way they flitted from me to the floor. I met him at Big John's before I started working there. James put some old CCR thing on the jukebox and danced on the dock. I joined him and the two of us established Big John's dance floor there and then. The next day, Big John had Scug sledgehammer away half the tables and benches formerly nailed into the dock itself to make room for dancing.

Jimmy and I had started a tradition, for the bar and ourselves. Every weekend we danced on that dock. We sat at the far end of the pier with out feet in the water talking. He told me about Kuwait, but only a little, or what seemed like a little to me. I told him about Delilah, Aunt Tabitha, the craft. To my relief, he didn't mind that I was a pagan. I think he might have a had some of it in himself, in fact.

He worried me. Jimmy came in once in rough shape. I tried to talk to him, but when he saw me he turned and got back in his boat. Later that night, in the early morning when I returned home, I lit a sick of incense on the flat river stone I use for an altar and prayed for him. Sometimes in our late-night talks he would look up at the stars that shone so clearly over the water, and say that we were all fire and dust. That everything was fire and dust.

I loved Jimmy but I knew it was doomed from the first moment. We made love the first time on a blanket in his backyard after a party at Big John's while the moon faded to her house and the stars turned as though time were nothing but the great unending wheel of the sky. After the second night I stayed with him, I knew he was going away from me. He lay there awake for a long time. I could feel it.

He went away from everyone. I could love him when he was off guard enough not to think about calling himself James instead of Jimmy. In those times, when he forgot himself, he was a wonderful man. Sentimental and sweet. He picked me all the flowers in his scrabble backyard, the dandelions and some azaleas that survived even though he never tended them. But he became uneasy. He threw away the things that would have made him happy, always reaching for more. I hope I was one of those things—at least, I hope that he loved me when he was himself. Maybe when he realizes his mistake I won't be too old to give him another chance.

This is the memory of him I keep: it was Jimmy's birthday at Big John's not long after he was back from the middle east. His arms and face were still dark from the desert sun, his old Braves cap still a part of him then. He bought round after round. Every time someone called out birthday wishes, he yelled back, lifted the bottle, kissed me while the people cheered. The party erupted onto the dock. We danced and Big John blared his old record collection over the outside speakers. I put my arms on Jimmy's shoulders and felt the sweat on his neck. He whispered promises to marry me, hopes to be with me our whole lives long. There, bathed in full-moon glow, I believed him. I knew enough to know he meant it. Later, that Jimmy faded away, and by the end I didn't have Jimmy anymore. I didn't even have James.

Jennifer said, "That's a hell of a thing to tell someone right before their wedding."

"Joseph isn't like Jimmy. Anyway, you would know if he was—doomed love is an unmistakable feeling." Mabby thought, and said very gently, "There's always danger in love. Or always risk."

"I know that."

"I know you do."

They rode. The sun hung overhead, baking the aluminum boat along with its flowers and passengers. Mabby piloted to the shore of a small island in the lake covered with tall, shading pines. Soft beds of pine needles covered the ground, perfect bedding for deer if any lived there. The two women grounded the boat and climbed out. They explored some, peering through the boughs at the lake houses on one side, close by, and the heads or stumps of flooded cypress trees above the water on the other. They heard a loud creaking and looked up to see a bald eagle leaving its huge nest, gliding after two flaps of its great wings. As they walked they discovered a boulder big enough to climb onto and rest. The stone was cool from the shade and they lay on it head to foot cooling themselves.

Perhaps both together had the idea to wait out the heat of the day on the island. Although gusts of hot, humid air flew by every now and again, the shade and the rock kept them cool enough. They drifted in and out of light sleep as the sunrays breaking through the pine branches crept east to west. After a time, they both lie awake, listening for the other but not needing the other to speak. Mabby did speak, saying, "I have one more story to tell you."

My mother died when I was little. It's funny how quickly we forget someone's face—how the lines and shadows fade into feeling, into sound, into something like a smell we can't quite remember. For me, it's the lapping of water. The scent of waves touching a worn steel boat.

They told me—the doctors, Aunt Tabitha—about my mother's accident. My child's mind imagined that my mother saw the car zooming towards her from the top left corner of her windshield and then everything faded to white. Tabitha told the doctors I could see the body. She warned me that my mother had been badly injured and would look different. I declined. Perhaps I felt like that white light had already erased her. I'm glad I didn't see her—I never would have forgotten the image of my mother torn apart.

After that I went to live with Aunt Tabitha, my mother's sister whose face was rougher but still beautiful. Tabitha never dined in town, never went to church, never shaved her legs. I wondered, with all these never's, where the always's were. She only gave me one: "Your Momma didn't leave, she just changed, and she'll always keep an eye on her baby." Tabitha told me that every night before bed.

Tabitha baked, just for us two, every day. Biscuits in the morning, cornbread from a cast-iron mold, cakes and cookies. That was one more always: a jar of fresh cookies.

She wasn't the type to listen, preferring to move. I didn't make a good talker either. The things I needed to get out didn't make sense to her or to anyone, not even me. They were brief memories of swaying Sunday pines, things that insisted upon themselves in my mind and I had no good reason why.

The evening I told her about Wicca, Tabitha and I nibbled hoe cakes, me drinking tea and her dipping cornbread in buttermilk as I explained everything.

"There's older women that do this stuff?" she asked.

"Yes, all ages. At least, the pictures in the book make it seem that way."

"I thought it was a young folks' thing."

"It's only a few thousand years old, Aunt T."

The women were quiet as they stirred and fully awoke and returned to the boat. Its metal was still warm but bearable. Jennifer climbed in and Mabby pushed off, using the momentum to tip-toe across the gunwale on one side to the stern seat before the boat tipped, a maneuver that made Jennifer laugh with the skill and silliness of it. Mabby backed the laden craft and turned it again into the channel she knew by heart. Mabby laughed too. They drove on nearly to the highway bridge laughing.

I finally decided to look for work. The fancy restaurant on the highway rejected me. Maybe they didn't like the shorts I showed up in, or the owners had heard of me at church. There was no mistaking a name like mine. Then I did what I should have done to begin with and applied at Big John's.

It was around afternoon when I showed up, the bar filled with retirees and kids on summer break. Big John was drunk, but that was unremarkable.

"You need a job?" he asked, and before I could answer, "You know how to work a cash register?"

"Sure," I said. How hard could it be?

"You from around here?" He asked, not looking at me but making a barbeque sandwich.

"Across the lake. I live with my aunt, Tabitha Woodrow."

"What'd you say your name was?"

"Maybellene Melissa Guthrie. You might know me as Mabby."

He did. Big John turned wide eyes to me and his beard inched onto his face while his eyebrows bent to meet it. "You're a witch."

"Yes, sir. Wiccan, though, not the other kind."

He tried to figure out what the other kind was. "All right. You wear shorts like that when you come in, you're hired."

I knew many of the people who came to the bar and I got to meet others, rich and poor alike. Three old men joked with me over their spades game. The linemen looked sideways at me, whispering about that origami crane.

On slow days I sat with Scug, Big John's relative from somewhere, listening to him sing his hillbilly songs. I tried to get Kyle to come to the bar, but he said in the same tone each time, "It would show a lack of prudence for a man of the Lord to be caught—" he drew out caaaught—"at such a place."

One day I said to Big John, "Hey boss."

"Yeah."

"Mind if my friend gets married on your dock?"

"They buy beer?"

"Yes."

"Suits me fine."

And that is how I secured your wedding venue.

The two laughed as they passed under the highway bridge and pulled the john boat alongside Big John's dock and moored it. Anne, Lilith, and a few of the others stood by to help decorate and they spent the early afternoon lining the dock with rows of flowers along all the rails, decking the posts with bouquets. By the end the dock did look like paradise, if one ignored the shack of the bar behind, whose ancient tin Coors ad rose above all.

The women hugged and parted ways. Jennifer made the comment that maybe handfasting wasn't as stressful as a wedding somehow, and they discussed this a moment, but it was only so they could remain together a little longer. They hugged, then went home to get ready.

Mabby unmoored her boat and turned it to the channel and piloted north. She fought the urge she often felt to dive into the water, to swim there in the deep middle of things.

The ceremony was set for that evening. Jennifer drove to meet Mabby there, and saw protesters before she parked.

A dozen men and women stood holding signs painted with Bible verses, or Jennifer thought they were, since they bore the words "witch" and "hell" and "satan." It being a Thursday night there wasn't anyone else much around, so the protesters stood like sentries of some court of judgment. Their leader, a small blonde man in a red blazer, paced before them, his hands on his hips pushing back his jacket. Jennifer had the feeling that while they may not have been waiting for her, when she appeared in her black dress with purple trim, her bag of ritual items, the sight would be stir them up. She sat in her car, fighting back anger at having that day she'd planned for months invaded. For the Goddess' sake, she thought, I knew these people were around here, but why do I have to meet them today? Jennifer sat with her hands gripping the wheel, that awful crew framed in her front windshield, her vision blurring. Then Mabby appeared.

Her friend rounded the corner, saw them, and the plain rage in her movements made the protesters step back. It took a moment to register with them that this tall, tattooed woman in her wild skirt and flowing hair was unmistakably of the witch crowd. Perhaps some of them hadn't believed that the thing they were protesting was real. The preacher raised a finger and launched into a condemnation of witchcraft and sin, his people crying out their support, until Mabby grabbed him by the lapels of his jacket.

She stood several inches taller than him. Jennifer hadn't noticed just how muscled her friend's arms were—from long hours of paddling, perhaps, or simply a life lived outdoors. The crowd hushed. Jennifer, in fear of what they might do, opened her door and ran to Mabby.

Her friend, holding the preacher up on his toes, said to him, "This is a wedding, a wedding you're disrupting."

The preacher said, though his breath seemed short, "A wedding is of God, young woman, but this abomination—"

"No, this is love, and don't you say that God is love? Hell, they're even straight." Mabby looked at the crowd as though just then seeing them. She called out, "What is wrong with you?" None responded. "You're all being awful and you should leave this minute so my friend can get married to the man she loves."

The preacher gurgled something and Mabby hissed "Shut up, Randy."

The protesters remained silent. It seemed like they hadn't actually expected anything to come of their protest, much less to meet the persons they protested. As they wavered, Mabby said with calmer conviction, "You can go. You've said what you needed to. There's no more obligation."

A big ruddy-faced man turned. The rest turned as well, moving to cars with their signs on their shoulders.

Mabby let down the preacher. He smoothed his jacket. Mabby said, "I can't believe you did this."

"We had to. We couldn't sit by in the face of witchcraft."

Mabby sighed. The heat of anger no longer came off her but instead some grave disappointment. She said, "You could have chosen to be decent instead of doing whatever the hell this was."

The preacher picked up his sign and said, "The Lord will judge every idle word, Miss Guthrie."

"Whatever Lord there is will judge your heart."

The two, preacher and witch, looked at one another and Jennifer wondered how these adversaries had come to be; how her friend Mabby and this odd preacher who spoke almost apologetically about his terrible obligations wound up, as people, gazing at one another like king and queen over their respective pawns. Then the preacher left and it was only the murmur of guests on the dock, the buzz of engines on the lake.

Mabby turned to Jennifer. "Are you okay?"

"Yes, yes, I had no idea—"

"I didn't either. Randy and his people seem to always show up the moment everyone's forgotten about them."

"You know what guy?"

Mabby's lips were tight. "The wanderer cannot always choose whom she meets along the path."

"Thanks, Confucius."

Mabby relaxed. "Come on, it's ready."

Arrangements of pink roses hung from the columns with garlands of honeysuckle—the others must have added yet more flowers during the day. Before Jennifer could glimpse more than the edge of the crowd gathered there, the coven pulled her aside, checking hair, makeup, holding up a mirror, asking her again and again if she were all right after having to walk past the protest. A little overwhelmed by so much care, Jennifer said yes, she was fine, and they asked her if she was ready. With a deep breath, she said yes. Mabby passed burning sage before her and together they murmured the initial prayers, quiet and intimate in that already excited party.

The coven made their circle at the end of the dock, spreading offerings to the four directions. The dried leaves floated around them on the calm water. Red August light spread and floated with those herbs and with the smoke from the altar, waving on the gentle passing wakes. Mabby sang one of the hymns that she and Delilah wrote, a plaintive but happy lilting piece. When Jennifer and Joseph kissed they were silhouetted in a halo of light, set apart for that moment from all the world, separate spirits of warm fire.

Even Lilith cried.

The reception packed Big John's dock with forty friends and fewer family. Big John wore a dinner jacket over his t-shirt as he passed bottle after bottle through the crowd. People danced to the LP's Tabitha brought from home. Booze and hippie skirts all over again, like the parties Mabby had described and which Jennifer was too embarrassed to admit she'd never attended. Jennifer danced with Joseph, with Mabby, with Anne, with so many people she lost track. Drunk silly dancing. Joseph beamed, telling her how beautiful it all was. Lilith stood with her perfect posture the whole time, talking with the less mobile of Anne's friends. As Mabby walked by once, Lilith rubbed her shoulder, that same motherly gesture as before, and told her how well she sang. By that time Mabby was too happy or loopy for it to bother her. She said thanks and walked on.

Later, the sounds of the party still loud behind her, Mabby stood by herself on the dock looking over the blue-topped water, sad only to be missing Delilah. She would have loved it. Probably she would have done a better job with the decorations. They would have sung together. Florescent light from the dock swayed on the quiet lake before her. Wood and water;

solid ground and deep-running chance. Booze, a little envy but a lot of pride for Jennifer, and Mabby missed her best friend. She leaned out over the nighttime ripples and saw herself broken into wild fractal waves.

When she looked back, Mabby saw her mother. Later she thought it was a dream—but what difference did that make? Her mother was there. Light from the water soaked into the folds of the dress she wore, a silk flower child thing embroidered with blue flowers at the neck. She looked as young as in the picture beside Mabby's bed, stood with such wise confidence that her daughter felt foolish beside her. There was a gentleness in those deep, wonderful eyes that made Mabby want to run to her, beg to be held. Mabby watched her, not wanting to break the spell, until Big John or somebody shot a firework over the dock and it exploded into the sky. They both looked up to see the sparks, a new universe of stars. When Mabby looked back, she was gone. And the party was there, Jennifer and Joseph dancing, Anne chatting with Aunt Tabitha. Mabby wiped her face with the back of her hand and joined them, dancing with those people of her life, all of them over the water.

about the author

Jackson Culpepper grew up in Georgia, whose red hills and swamps shaped these stories. Since then, he has lived in Southern Appalachia, the mountain west, and the desert southwest. Songs on the Water was his fiction thesis at the University of South Carolina's MFA program. His work has appeared in *Armchair/Shotgun, Cartridge Lit,* and most recently in *Identity Theory.* He currently serves as the poet laureate of the progressive First Baptist Church of Denver, where his poems have been set to music and performed. He lives and teaches first-year English at several community colleges in the Denver, Colorado area.

At Wayfarer Books we believe poetry is the language of the earth. We believe words, shaped like rivers through wild places, can change the shape of the world. We publish poets and writers and renegades who stand outside of mainstream culture—poets, essayists, and storytellers whose work might withstand the scrutiny of crows and coyotes, those who are cryptic and floral, the crepuscular, and the queer-at-heart. We are more than just a publisher but a community of writers. Our mission is to produce books that can serve as a compass and map to all wayfarers through wild terrain.

WWW.WAYFARERBOOKS.ORG